Donated By: Kenyon Noble Lumber Hardware

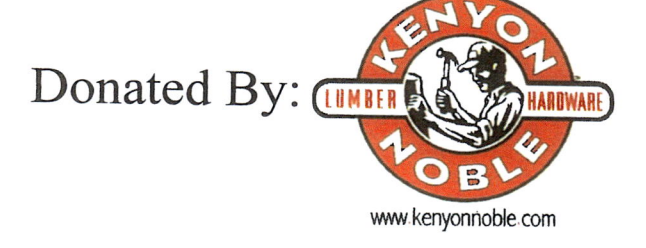

www.kenyonnoble.com

ARIZONA RANGER

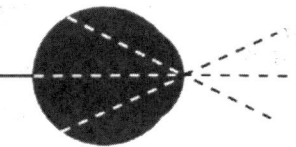

**This Large Print Book carries the
Seal of Approval of N.A.V.H.**

ARIZONA RANGER

A. SCOTT LESLIE

CENTER POINT LARGE PRINT
THORNDIKE, MAINE

This Center Point Large Print edition
is published in the year 2021 by arrangement with
Golden West Literary Agency.

Copyright © 1938 by Leslie A. Scott.
Copyright © renewed 1966 by Leslie A. Scott.

All rights reserved.

Originally published in the US by
Robert Speller Publishing Corporation.

This is a work of fiction. The characters, incidents,
and dialogues are products of the author's imagination
and are not to be construed as real.

The text of this Large Print edition is unabridged.
In other aspects, this book may vary
from the original edition.
Printed in the United States of America
on permanent paper.
Set in 16-point Times New Roman type.

ISBN: 978-1-64358-815-5 (hardcover)
ISBN: 978-1-64358-819-3 (paperback)

The Library of Congress has cataloged this record under
Library of Congress Control Number: 2020948315

ARIZONA RANGER

1

"Hoss, it's him!"

The big golden sorrel nodded his head wisely, as if agreeing with his master. He craned his glossy neck and peered down the winding trail toward where a tiny dot rose and fell. It was a mere dark blob on the white ribbon of road, growing swiftly larger as the seconds passed.

Ranger Rance Hatfield also watched that growing dot. Watched it with much greater interest than did his horse.

"Comin' nawth on the Zacara trail like we was told," muttered the Ranger. "This is gonna be jest too easy!"

He made sure, however, that his guns were loose in their carefully worked and oiled Cheyenne holsters. After all, Cavorca, the outlaw, was not a person to trifle with.

On came the horseman. Hatfield on his hilltop, hidden by dense growths of mesquite, watched and waited. Above him a huge condor-vulture sailed and wheeled. Rance noted it absently, his mind intent on the horseman.

"Yeah, that's his big black stallion, *El Rey*," he told the sorrel a little later. "I'd know that cayuse in a million—he's the—"

Movement birthed in the mesquite back of the

Ranger. With a silken swish something coiled snakily from the shadows. A tight loop snugged over his wide shoulders like a noose of golden light. There was a fast little "Zip!" and Hatfield left the saddle as if he had taken unto himself wings. He hit the ground with terrific force and for a moment lay stunned. Around and around him wound the rope, until he was utterly helpless, trussed up like a pig for market.

"What the hell?" he stuttered dazedly to the dark face bending over him.

The face smiled thinly and vanished. For long minutes Hatfield lay silent and motionless, his body slowly numbing as the rope cut into his flesh. His senses were coming back and his brain was alert.

Like distant castanets, the click of hoofs drifted through the hot, still air. Rance strained his ears to listen.

"Jest one hoss," he muttered; "that'll be Cavorca, sho' as hell! Damn that sidewinder, anyhow! He's slippery'r than a greased snake on ice; and he allus seems to get all the breaks. S'pose it was one of his sneaky men what hawgtied me."

The clicking hoofs ragged off to a shamble, ceased. Rance heard Spanish remarks tossed to and fro. He craned his head sideways as footsteps approached.

"*Buenos dias, senor*," purred a voice musical as sunlight dropping down a waterfall.

Rance looked up at the man standing over him and was reminded of something he had once heard a traveling preacher read from the Bible:

"... *in all Israel there was none to be so much praised for his beauty: from the sole of his foot to the crown of his head there was no blemish in him.*"

"Jest the same, spite of all his good looks," muttered the ex-cowboy, "Absolom had his own brother murdered and worried his pore old Dad gray-headed with his hell raisin'! And he didn't have a damn thing on this horned toad!"

Manuel Cavorca smiled a slow, thin smile, revealing teeth that flashed white and even in the sunlight.

"You speak with yourself, *senor*?" he lisped. "Droll! And most strange you think! You think, ha! to trap Manuel Cavorca, eh? Set your traps on the mountain crests, *Senor Ranger!* Place your snares in the arms of the morning mists! Weave you a net of the twilight winds and bait it with sunbeams! Ha! then you will catch Manuel Cavorca, perhaps!"

Silently the lean, bronzed American stared into the eyes of the bandit. Manuel Cavorca, tall, lithe, with hair like the sun-gold and eyes as blue as the summer skies, stared back. Stared back until those chill gray eyes seemed to burn holes into his brain. Despite his efforts his gaze wavered. Murderous rage wiped all the marvellous beauty from his face and left it hideous. His perfectly molded lips writhed back from his perfect teeth in a coyote-grimace. The china-whites of his eyes reddened with passion. His musical voice harshed to a vulture-croak.

"Take him!" he rasped to the dark, silent men who stood at the edge of the mesquite.

Quickly the dark men closed in. They unwound the lariat, jerked Rance to his feet and bound his hands behind him.

"To the top of the cliff," ordered Cavorca.

With cocked rifles prodding him, Rance stumbled through the mesquite and up a winding trail. On the lip of a dizzy height he was told to stop. He stood quietly gazing down at the black fangs of rock two hundred feet below.

A loop was flung about his shoulders and drawn snug. Cavorca gave him a shove and an instant later he was dangling over the cliff edge with two hundred feet of nothing at all beneath him. The men on the cliff quickly paid out the rope. They fastened the end securely to a jutting knob of stone. Manuel Cavorca leaned over and stared at the man swinging helpless against the cliff.

"*Adios*, *Senor* Ranger," he called. "We shall *not* meet again. Soon our friends the vultures will pluck out your eyes, so that you will not be able to see them feeding upon your body; but doubtless you will feel them. *Adios*!"

A peal of silvery, mocking laughter echoed

against the canyon walls. Hoofs clicked away into the distance.

"I'd oughta knowed somethin' was hid in the mesquite—the way that vulture acted," Rance growled. "Wonder if the damn things *will* tackle a man while he's still alive?"

Soon the great condor-vultures came swooping down to investigate more closely the thing that hung nearly motionless against the cliff. Rance wriggled his body convulsively and shouted. The huge birds sheered off, only to return; Rance could feel the wind from their mighty wings.

Again and again he shouted, until his throat was raw and his voice cracking. The rope loop was cutting into his flesh like an eating flame. His body was growing numb. His brain was swimming.

"If I pass out the damn things'll tackle me," he kept telling himself. "They're afraid so long as I keep makin' a racket, but they know I'm helpless like a steer with a broken leg. They're jest waitin'!"

The sun was crawling down the western sky, a ball of flaming brass whose fierce rays drank the moisture from the Ranger's body and set up a terrific thirst. His mouth was like crackled leather, his blackening tongue was pressing against his teeth, his lips were parched and bleeding. Fiery ropes of pain coiled about his body and lashed his brain. He began to mutter incoherently. Waves of color stormed and pulsed before his eyes. The whistling wings of the vultures no longer had power to rouse him.

A great snapping beak, scant inches from his face, brought him back to full consciousness with a jerk. He shouted hoarsely. The vulture swerved sharply away.

It seemed to Rance that the echo was more than usually loud and clear.

"Sounds almost like somebody else hollerin'," he panted. "It—holy Peter! It *is* somebody!"

A voice was ringing up to him from below the cliff—a clear, musical voice.

"Hold on a little longer," it said, "I'm coming up to you."

Minutes passed, minutes that seemed hours to the almost delirious Ranger. The voice sounded again, above him this time—

"Isn't there any way you can get your hands loose?"

"No," Rance called back, his voice a rasping croak, "they're tied behind me—tight."

Craning his neck sideways, he stared up the cliff. Leaning over the edge, he could make out the face of a girl framed in a cluster of short dark curls that the strong up-draft from the canyon whipped back from her white forehead and her creamily tanned cheeks. He could see that her eyes were big and dark.

"I'm coming down," she called.

The face vanished. Two trim little feet in high-heeled boots thrust over the edge. In another instant she was scrambling down the rope.

"Hey!" shouted Rance in frenzied protest, "this rope won't hold us both! You'll get yourself killed! Go back!"

She gave no heed to his frantic words. Down she came, her trim little form scraping and bruising against the cliff face. She reached the Ranger, kicked her feet skillfully aside and slid down until she was gripping the rope just above the loop that was drawn tight below his shoulders. Between her white little teeth she held an open knife.

With the greatest care, she braced her feet upon the Ranger's, let go the rope with one hand and gripped the knife with the other.

"I'm going to cut your hands loose," she told him.

Setting the knife edge against the tough rawhide thong she sawed away. Barely able to reach his bound wrists, she could put but little pressure on the knife and progress was torturingly slow. Rance could hear her breath coming in choking gasps, could feel her slight body jerk and quiver with strain.

"I'm getting it," she panted. "Just another cut or two and I'll have it."

A great shadow hovered over the pair for an instant, weaved aside and returned, closer.

"Them damn buzzards are back!" Rance panted.

He shouted as loudly as he could. The shadow tumbled away with a hoarse croak of disappointment. The girl's hand moved in faltering jerks.

Rance swelled his muscles and strained with all his strength against the thongs. He could feel the blood trickling from where they were cutting into his flesh like red-hot wires. He set his teeth and put forth a final mighty effort.

He felt the rawhide stretch. His hands flew apart. The girl's feet slipped from his and for a terrible instant she swung dizzily by one hand. Rance gripped her with almost numb fingers and held her until she had secured a better hold.

The Ranger's hands were free, but his arms, from shoulder to elbow, were still penned to his sides.

"I'll have to cut the loop," the girl said. "Can you reach up far enough to grasp the rope?"

Feeling was flowing back into his fingers and he managed to hook them around the strand of rawhide that pressed so tightly against his chest.

"Go ahaid," he told her, "but be shore you cut in the right place. If you cut above the slip-knot, I'll be jest like a feller tryin' to hold hisself up by his boot straps."

Swiftly the keen blade ate through the rope. Rance felt the pressure against his arms loosen.

An instant later he plunged sickeningly downward.

He brought up with a terrific jerk, clutching and clawing, the rope slipping through his fingers. The fuzzy cut end was in his hand before he checked his horrible slide toward death. Just above his head dangled the girl.

"Climb on up," Rance told her, "I'll be right behind you."

A gasping little cry answered him: "I can't! My arms aren't strong enough! All I can do is hold on!"

Rance Hatfield's mouth set grimly, but his eyes gleamed with admiration.

"Never stopped to think about that when she started down," he applauded. "That's nerve for you, feller!"

"Keep right on hangin' on," he called cheerily, "I'll get us both up quicker'n a steer can switch its tail in fly time. Soon as I climb up to you, let go the rope and wrap yore arms *round* my neck."

"You can't climb with me hanging onto you," protested the girl.

"Don't arg'fy with me!" barked Rance. "Do as yo're told!"

The girl obeyed, winding her slim arms about his neck, letting her body hang down over his shoulders.

"Jest keep real still, now," Rance warned her.

Slowly, painfully, he began to climb the rope.

It was less than twenty feet to the lip of the cliff, but to Rance it seemed twenty miles. The girl's weight, small at first, grew to a terrific burden. The fierce heat of the sun rays beating back from the cliff face sapped his already draining strength. His fingers seemed numb rods of soft lead. His arms were a vast fiery ache. To slide one hand above the other became a task that called for every atom of will power he possessed.

Inch by crawling inch. Then his gripping hand would slide back and it seemed to him that he had lost all the distance gained. The croaks of the wheeling vultures became hoarse shouts of triumph. Rance gritted his teeth.

"Not yet, you sky-runnin' coyotes!" he rasped. "I'll fool you this time!"

The score of feet had shrunk to less than half of that. Rance's eyes gleamed with hope; then the gleam turned to a wild glare of apprehension.

The cliff edge where the rope swung over was sharp and jagged. The knife-like stone was fraying the line as it jerked back and forth to the Ranger's progress. His horrified eyes saw the little strands part and curl up like the lips of an angry dog. Another and another, until it seemed only a mere thread supported the heavy burden; and that last thread was swiftly fraying away.

With the strength of despair, Rance surged upward. He flung a madly questing hand over the cliff edge as the rope parted, his fingers closed about a knob of stone and clung desperately.

"Save yoreself, quick!" he gulped to the girl.

Agile as a cat, she clutched the cliff edge and hurled herself sideways and up. Rolling over onto her face she gripped the Ranger's wrist and held on grimly. Rance got the fingers of his other hand around the knob of stone and drew himself over the edge.

Panting, exhausted, almost unconscious, he lay, sweat pouring from him, trembling in every limb.

"I'll get water!" exclaimed the girl, whipping up the hat she had dropped when she started down the rope.

She came back with it slopping over the crown in a silvery trickle. Rance drank it to the last drop, renewed strength flowing through his veins with every swallow. He got to his feet unsteadily, working his still numb fingers.

"Ma'am," he said, "if somebody'd told me last week that angels went 'round dressed in boots and wool shirts and ridin' pants, I'da called him a liar. Right now I'd shake hands with him and agree he was plumb observin'."

The girl dimpled up at him, her white little teeth flashing in a merry smile.

"Well, a set of wings would certainly have come in handy a little while ago," she laughed. "How did you ever come to be hanging around here that way? A bet or something?"

Rance grinned a trifle ruefully. "Uh-huh, and

I lost. A little friend of mine named Manuel Cavorca said I'd stretch a rope 'fore he ever did. Guess he had the right of it, but his time's comin'!"

The smile had left the girl's face and she was gazing at the Ranger with troubled eyes.

"You're not one of Cavorca's men, are you?" she asked.

"Nope," Rance assured her, "I sho' ain't."

"But w-why did he do this thing?"

"Well, you see, Ma'am," Rance hesitated, "I was—was lookin' for Cavorca. He—he sorta found me 'stead of me findin' him."

"But why were you looking for him?"

Again Rance hesitated. He was not given to discussing official business with strangers, not even strangers as attractive as this one. But, after all, he reasoned, the girl had saved his life. And what harm could come from answering her question?

"Cavorca is a bandit, wanted by the law, and I am Rance Hatfield, an Arizona Ranger detailed to run him down," he said simply.

He stared in astonishment at the effect his statement had.

The color drained from the girl's rose-red lips, leaving them gray and drawn. The light went out in her eyes, then suddenly blazed forth like a lightning flash. One trim little hand hovered over the gun slung at her hip and for an instant Rance thought she was going to draw on him. The hand dropped, she turned and very deliberately walked to the cliff edge and gazed down at the jagged rocks ten-score feet below. Then she turned back to face the Ranger again and spoke, her voice flat and toneless:

"Well, anyhow, I kept the vultures from getting poisoned!"

She began to laugh, wildly, almost hysterically!

"And I risked my life to save Rance Hatfield, the Rangers' ace killer, their prize gunman! Rance Hatfield!"

Suddenly her slender right hand flashed out. A quirt slashed Rance across the face—a stinging, welt-raising blow.

Before Rance could say a word she fled, blindly, stumbling, down the steep slope toward the mesquite flat. A moment later he heard the click of hoofs dying away in the distance!

2

Still badly shaken by his terrifying experience, Rance stumbled back to the trail. He eyed the winding white ribbon with distaste. Cowboy-like, he hated to walk; nor were his tight, high-heeled boots suited for batting it through sand and over rocks.

But walk he must. To the south, just beyond a range of low hills, was the barbed-wire fence that marked the Arizona-Mexico border. To the north were more hills, and the Blanton ranch. Cavorca was headed for the Blanton ranch. A few muttered words overheard while the bandits were binding him had told Hatfield that. He braced his belt and headed north.

The Blanton ranch was a big spread whose southern edge in places lapped the border. Old man Blanton, it was said, kept money in the ranch-house, a great deal of it. He also kept a number of straight-shooting punchers in his employ.

"And," growled Rance Hatfield, stumping an aching toe against the hard side of a rock, "if Blanton hadn't sent most all his men nawth with that big trail herd day-'fore-yest'day, Cavorca wouldn't never take a chance at raidin' the Bar-B. That hellion knows ev'thing what goes on this side the line 'fore it even happens, damn him!"

The sun sank in riotous red and burnished gold. The lovely blue dusk draped the hills in royal robes and marched away cross the sky. The figure of the man trudging along the trail seemed to grow smaller and more lonely. The black hand of night closed upon him and he vanished.

Beyond the hills to the north a red glow beat against the sky. Rance Hatfield saw it and quickened his pace. It grew in intensity, flared up fiercely, sank and then flared again.

"The hellions has set fire to the straw stacks and the stables," growled the Ranger. "Next'll be the ranch-house."

A faint crackling, as of the distant flames, came to his ears.

"Blanton and whoever's with him in the house is puttin' up a good scrap," he panted. "Jest listen to them guns go!"

As he topped a final hill, the gunfire roared up to him. The ranch-house stood out starkly in the light of the burning stables, its roof a-smoke in a dozen places.

Flames flashed and spurted in the grove surrounding the building. Other sparky jets answered from the shadowy walls. Rance Hatfield, quivering with excitement, watched the battle from his hilltop.

"Blanton ain't got more'n two, three men in theah with him," the Ranger quickly estimated.

"Cavorca's got a dozen, mebbe more. Soon as that roof gets to blazin' good, the fellers in the house'll hafta come out. Cavorca'll mow 'em down like jackrabbits. I'm gonna try and get closer."

Cautiously he slipped down the hill. Unarmed, he could afford to take few chances. He reached the edge of the grove and paused, listening intently. Horses were snorting only a few yards distant. On hands and knees, Rance crept toward them, saw them dimly outlined against the light.

"Jest one man left to watch 'em," he breathed exultantly. "Now if I get somethin' like a break—"

The watchman was intent on the battle going on at the edge of the grove. He heard nothing, saw nothing as death leaped at him from the shadows. Fingers like rods of nickel-steel closed about his throat. His head was twisted around. A tremendous blow crashed against his jaw and he went limp.

Rance eased the Mexican to the ground, slipping a tangle of reins from his stiffened fingers. There was some snorting from the horses, but the affair had been handled so quickly and with such little fuss that the bronks were not really alarmed. Rance's soothing whispers quickly quieted them.

"Six," the Ranger counted. "Another bunch around heah somewheah—t'other side the grove, chances are. Well, this'll be enough for what I want."

Up the hill he led the horses. With grim satisfaction he noted that one was Cavorca's giant black, *El Rey*—The Lightning Flash. Not a bad trade for his sorrel!

Rance could feel the hard outlines of revolvers in one of *El Rey*'s saddlebags. Exultantly he drew forth his own belt and Colts. Cavorca had evidently intended them for his own future use.

"You'll sho' get the hot end of one if I can jest manage to draw a bead on you, you murderin' sidewinder!" the Ranger growled as he mounted *El Rey*.

Guns continued to crack in the grove. The ranch-house roof was burning nicely now. The raiders whooped as the flames leaped up.

"Hi-yi-yi-yi-yi! Give 'em hell, boys! Give 'em hell!"

From somewhere up the hill back of the ranch-house came that wild yell. The crackle of six-shooters dinned through it. And a rousing drum of racing hoofs.

Back through the grove blundered the raiders. Shouts of consternation arose from those who found their horses missing. Their mounted comrades charged toward them and there was a wild tangle of rearing horses and cursing men as the two groups came together. The yelling and shooting still stormed down the hill.

In a mad panic, Cavorca's bandits fled for the border. Rance Hatfield sent a final fusillade of shots after them. The horses he had driven down the hill in front of him milled about through the grove, snorting and pawing. Old man Blanton poured questions from the ranch-house door. His two sons were busy pouring water on the roof.

Many hours later, Rance Hatfield sat in Ranger headquarters and talked with Captain Morton. Morton, a slender, well groomed little man with a pleasant face and cold gray eyes, regarded his crack Ranger with the suspicion of a twinkle.

"Well," he said when Rance had finished his story, "it looks to me like you and Cavorca jest about broke even on this petickler deal. He got yore hoss and you got his. He busted up yore little scheme to grab him off and you busted up his to grab off old man Blanton's money. What I'd like to know is wheah does that gal fit inter all this? You got any idea?"

Rance shook his head. "Nope," he replied, touching with a tentative finger the still tender welt across his bronzed cheek, "she's sho' got me guessin'. She was all friendly like till I told her I was a Ranger. When I said it was Cavorca what tied me up for buzzard bait, I could see it bothered her a lot; but when I said 'Ranger!' Mamma mine! did she go on the prod! Funny!"

"Well, she saved you a trip across to the Big Spread, anyhow," said Morton. "Touchin' on

Cavorca—we got another tip for you to work on. He's yore meat and I'm passin' the job to you. Now listen to this—"

Rance listened intently, and voiced an objection. "But why Crazy Hoss Gulch?" he questioned. "Why not Skull Canyon? Or wheah the Zacara trail runs through that spur of the Tonto Hills jest this side the line?"

Morton shook his head definitely. "I hadda talk with the bigwigs," he replied, "and it was 'greed that Crazy Hoss Gulch was the best place. The bullion train'll hafta go through theah. Cavorca knows it and that's wheah he'll wait. The train might go through Skull Canyon, and then again it might take the nawth trail. Cavorca wouldn't have no way of knowin' if they decided to change their minds the last minute."

Rance was not convinced. "That sidewinder knows ev'thin'," he growled pessimistically, "and doin' the thing nobody 'spects him to do is what he's plumb strong on. But yore the boss. Crazy Hoss Gulch she is."

3

There are ghosts in Skull Canyon—if you believe in ghosts. Perhaps there are whether you believe in them or not. That eerie wail that floats between the gloomy walls may be the hunting call of a hungry cougar. And it may be the tortured cry of some poor devil's spirit who met a bloody end there and left his bones to bleach white beneath the fierce Arizona sun.

For thrice a score of years there have been white bones in Skull Canyon. The relics of murderous encounters between outlaws and smugglers. Or of the raids of marauding Apaches who swept down upon lonely prospectors. Geronimo used to pass that way. Curly Bill and John Ringo rode through Skull Canyon at the head of their lawless band. Skull Canyon knew Old Man Clanton and Dick Gray and Billy Lang in their heyday of evil.

Like none of these was the lone horseman who lounged easily in his saddle in the cool shade of the towering rock walls. Lithe and graceful, with clear blue eyes, clean cut features and crisp golden hair, he looked, in his picturesque garb, like a singularly handsome cowboy young in years and young in experience. His magnificent golden sorrel pawed impatiently and arched a graceful neck.

The rider's slim white hand tightened on the reins. The cruel Mexican bit jerked the horse's head up viciously. He snorted, reared and then stood trembling. Manuel Cavorca hissed a Spanish oath.

From far down the canyon came the faint click of hoofs. Cavorca straightened tensely in the saddle. A red gleam shot through his eyes. He drew his big pearl-handled sixes from their holsters, glanced at them, twirled the cylinders and dropped them back.

The sorrel moved forward at a walk. Cavorca raised his hand in a swift, furtive gesture.

From the tangled chaparral along the canyon rim a hand gestured in reply. Cavorca rode slowly down the canyon.

Nearer came the click of hoofs. Suddenly loud as the leading mules of the bullion train swung around a bend in the trail.

A man riding slightly in advance of the first mule glimpsed the one horseman. He held up his hand and the train jingled to a halt. The man rode forward, rifle ready.

"Howdy?" called Manuel Cavorca.

"Howdy," grunted the guard in reply, his eyes suspicious.

Cavorca rode on, open-faced, guileless. The guard relaxed a trifle.

"Wheah you headin' for, feller?" he asked.

"Huntin' strays," Cavorca replied. "I b'long

with the L-Bar-W, nawth of heah." (The guard knew the L-Bar-W was a big outfit that employed a number of men.)

"You notice any ramblin' beef critters the way you come?" asked Cavorca.

The guard had, he admitted. No, he hadn't noticed the brands.

Other armed men had ridden up by now, favoring the horseman with keen scrutinies. Cavorca played the part of a harmless cowpoke well. Their suspicions were allayed.

"Get goin' back theah," one called to the mule train.

Hoofs clicked. Harness jingled. Cavorca rode along the line of animals each bearing a rawhide *aparejo*, or pack sack, in which was stored its load of bullion. Heavily armed outriders along the flanks of the train searched rocks and coverts with keen eyes. They were taking no chances. Cavorca had a word of greeting for each, although often his answer was little more than a grunt. The last two nodded pleasantly.

Cavorca rode on a few paces, whirled the sorrel and jerked his guns. Shooting with both hands, he poured bullets into the backs of the men who had greeted him. They tumbled from their saddles and lay still. Cavorca fired at the men next in line.

Like echoes to his guns, rifles roared along the rim of the canyon. Flame spouted from the chaparral. A storm of lead swept the outriders from their saddles. The men riding ahead whirled their horses, and were shot down before they could raise their rifles. Skull Canyon was a shambles.

Back along the train raced Cavorca. He shot three wounded men, leaned from the saddle and clubbed another to death with his pistol barrel. His dark-faced bandits swarmed into the canyon. Working swiftly and expertly, they turned the bullion train and headed it back the way it had come, urging the frantic mules to panic flight. Once out of the canyon, they turned the train at almost right-angles and drove it toward the border.

Manuel Cavorca, his face that of an exultant fiend, dropped to the rear, peering, listening, searching the hilltops and canyon rims for possible pursuit.

Rance Hatfield and his troop of Rangers, waiting in distant Crazy Horse Gulch, straightened in their saddles as a faint crackle, like to the exploding of a pack of firecrackers, drifted to their ears. For a moment they listened intently; then Rance swore a vicious oath.

"I knowed it!" he shouted. "Skull Canyon! The hellions has drygulched the train theah! C'mon, boys, mebbe we'll be in time to grab 'em 'fore they make the line!"

Out of the Gulch surged the troop, hoofs drumming, horses snorting with excitement. The bronzed, grim-faced Rangers leaned low in their saddles, peering toward where the eastern mouth of Skull Canyon loomed misty and vague in the distance. The troop strung out as the better horses forged to the front.

Rance Hatfield, mounted on *El Rey*, steadily drew away from his men. The great black was a marvel of speed and endurance—the finest horse Rance had ever ridden. He entered into the spirit of the race as if he knew what it was all about. His hoofs beat back the echoes in a rattling roll of sound. His long black body seemed to fairly pour itself over the ground. Red-eyed, snorting, he slugged his big head above the bit and unreeled the ribbon of miles behind him.

Low in the west, the sun sent level red rays slanting across the prairie. They bathed a distant horseman in blood and fire. Rance Hatfield, peering into the glare, swore exultantly.

"That's him, hoss," he shouted to the black. "That's Cavorca on old Goldy, sho' as yore a foot high. He's ridin' rear guard. C'mon, put me in shootin' distance of that horned toad!"

El Rey snorted reply. His hoofs drummed faster. Flecks of foam spotted his shining coat. Stride by stride he closed the distance.

A grove, already purpled with shadows, loomed ahead. The sorrel vanished in the growth. Rance crouched lower but did not check the black.

"He won't take a chance on drygulchin' me

theah," reasoned the Ranger. "He'll figger the rest of the boys is clost behind. Go get him, hoss!"

Into the grove swept *El Rey*, his hoofs flinging back ragged echoes from the tree trunks. Rance loosened a gun in its holster, leaned still lower and searched the shadows. The dark-washed trunks drew closer to the trail.

Crash!

The great black horse turned a complete somersault, flinging his rider from him like a stone from a sling. He landed on his back, rolled over, and scrambled to his feet, snorting and trembling. He whickered querulously, swayed his head from side to side and limped to where Rance Hatfield lay white and silent. The rope, tautly stretched between two tree trunks, that had tripped him still hummed and vibrated; then the dying drum of hoofs fading away into the night.

El Rey's snorting breath in his ear aroused Rance. The Ranger sat up dizzily, rubbed an egg-sized lump on the side of his head and swore.

"Hoss, that greaser makes me feel like I was a monkey in a side show," he complained.

Shakily he got to his feet, examined the stallion and found him little the worse for his experience.

"That's two times for him," he told the animal, "but next time—"

4

Manuel Cavorca vanished below the line. The purple mountains of Mexico swallowed him up, and it appeared he intended to stay swallowed. They also swallowed his band of killers and a score of bullion laden mules. As Captain Morton said to Rance Hatfield:

"P'haps, after such a big haul, he decided to quit raidin' this side the border. Mebbe he's gonna reform and go straight."

"Uh-huh?" grunted Hatfield. "When that horned toad stops raisin' hell will be when he gets a overdose of lead poisonin' or dances on nothin' at the end of a rope."

Captain Morton meditated a moment. "Yore still on the lookout for Cavorca, of co'hse," he replied at length, "but it 'pears he's stayin' under cover for the time bein'. I want you to take a little run over to Coffin. Reports of killin's and robbin's and gen'ral hell-raisin' have been frequent from theah lately. The sheriff of Tonto county has his headquarters theah and they got a town marshal, too, but they don't seem to be handlin' the situation much. We gotta tip the jiggers what held up the Silver City stage last week is holed up theah. That'll be yore assignment; but we want a lineup on things in gen'ral at Coffin."

Rance found Coffin plenty "salty." The center of a big new gold strike, the town had mushroomed up in the very shadow of that forbidding region of jumbled hills and canyons known as The Black Hell. *El Infierno Negro* was a land of black rock and white water. The dark fangs of stone ripped against a hard brassy-blue sky from which poured heat like smoky water gushing from an inverted funnel. Vultures perched on the crags. Wolves slunk through the canyons. Outlaws perched or slunk, as the occasion called for. *El Infierno Negro* was a badman's paradise.

La Mesa Encantada, lying south and east of The Black Hell, was fine range land and covered by a number of big spreads.

Coffin, roaring and yammering with lusty life, sat in the borderland between the two regions. As a Lazy-D puncher told Rance:

"Look one way and things is purty as a drunk cowpoke's dream. Look the other way and she looks jest like that same work dodger feels next mawnin' when he's soberin' up."

Rance could see very little that might indicate "sobering up" that sun-splashed afternoon as he stabled his horse and proceeded to hunt out a square meal for himself.

A little restaurant presided over by a smiling Chinaman provided steak, huge quantities of fried potatoes, hot biscuits and coffee. The Ranger set to like a man who had known what it was to find good food scarce. Through a window he watched the colorful stream of life flowing up and down the straggling street.

Miners, bearded and brawny, swaggered by, their pockets bulging with sacks of "dust." Lean, bronzed cowboys high-heeled along, gazing about them with the quick, all-seeing glance of the plainsmen. Gamblers in long-tailed black coats, with expressionless faces, and derringers in their sleeves, eased their silent way through the crowd. Women with vivid lips and diamond-bright eyes that missed nothing that swayed past. Several evinced more than a casual interest in the tall, broad-shouldered Ranger who sat just inside the open window. Rance answered their greetings with a friendly but impersonal nod and smile that caused more than one painted "dance-hall girl" to look a trifle wistful as she left the window behind.

On the street again, Rance was caught up in the swirl and rush of lusty life. His pulses thrilled to the turmoil and excitement all around him. Coffin was a roaring gold-strike town with a pulse set to the tempo of exploding dynamite. Her hands were wet with sweat and blood. Curses and laughter tumbled together from her painted lips. There were no keys to the doors of her saloons, dance-halls and gambling hells. Men did not take the trouble to wind their watches. Time was not measured by days and hours but by events. Men talked gold and breathed gun smoke. Days of hard toil blended into nights of harder play. Sleep was looked upon as an unpleasant necessity.

"She's sho' a snortin' *pueblo*," Rance Hatfield admired as he stepped into a saloon. "Guess old Tombstone in the silver days didn't have nothin' on her. Now if we jest had a couple Doc Hollidays and a Wyatt Earp or two, with some Curly Bills and John Ringos throwed in for good measure!"

Rance had a drink of something that tasted like burning gunpowder and was like swallowing a buzz saw running at high speed.

"Prime whiskey, eh?" said the barkeep. "That's our own private stock."

Rance nodded. "Uh-huh, sorta mild. Give me 'nother one."

He downed the second drink and headed for the door. Up the street sounded a low thunder of drumming hoofs. Rance stepped out in time to see men scattering wildly, more wagons pulling onto the sidewalks. "What the hell's goin' on?" he wondered.

Down the street galloped six men mounted on splendid horses. Heavy revolvers swung from their cartridge belts. A rifle was thrust into the saddle scabbard of each. They wore a picturesque garb that was a combination of the flashy outfit of the Mexican *vaquero* and the just as striking but more serviceable "work clothes" of the American puncher.

Across the street from the saloon which Rance had just left they pulled the horses to a dancing halt, hitched them to a nearby rack and headed for the saloon. The Ranger eyed them with interest.

Tall, lithe, somewhat dark of complexion, with black hair and flashing black eyes, they were handsome men. All were young.

Rance Hatfield's black brows drew together in a perplexed frown as the group crossed the street.

"Ev'ry one of them jiggers looks alike and ev'one of them reminds me of somebody," he muttered. "I know darn well I ain't never seen none of them befo', but they make me feel like I have."

The six strangers entered the saloon. As Rance gazed after them thoughtfully, he heard a couple of men talking in back of him.

"It's the Gandara boys," said one. "They'll raise hell t'night. They allus does."

"Brothers?" asked the other men.

"Uh-huh," replied the first speaker. "Three-of-a-kind, a pair, and one to draw to."

"What the hell you talkin' about?" demanded the second man.

"Well," said the first speaker with a chuckle, "it's like this. Theah's Guilermo, the oldest. Then theah's the twins, Tomaso and Pedro, they come next. Then theah's the, what you call 'em? Oh, yeah, the triples, Fernando, Angel and Enrique. Theah was another boy in the family, I heard tell, but he left this section long time ago and sorta drifted outa sight."

"Mexicans, eh?"

"Nope. Americans—pure Spanish blood. Old Don Manuel Gandara got a land grant from the Mexican governor nigh onto a hundred yeahs ago, when Mexico and all this section b'longed to Spain. Family's allus lived heah. Our co'hts held the title was good and they own a gosh-awful big spread nawth of heah. Alfredo Gandara, them feller's pappy, is a fine old gent, but the boys is sorta wild."

Rance walked up the street, pondering what he had heard. The Gandaras had aroused his interest. Their bearing was proud, almost arrogant, as might be expected of descendants from the Spanish conquerors.

"Fine fellers us'ally, that kind," mused the Ranger, " 'less somethin' starts them off on the wrong foot. Then you can expect most anythin' from them, and the chances are then you'll get somethin' you don't expect."

Rance entered a small building marked "Sheriff's Office." A big fleshy man with handlebar moustaches and moth-eaten hair looked up from a table with a grunt. He wore a disgruntled expression and a shirt that needed washing. In a rickety chair beside the window sat a small twinkle-eyed individual hiding behind a grin.

"Howdy," said the Ranger, "I wanta see Sheriff Bethune."

"Ain't nothin' wrong with yore eyesight, is theah?" grunted the big man.

"Nope," replied Rance. "Ears is workin' good, too. Why?"

"You been lookin' at me the last couple minutes."

"Oh, so yore the sheriff. You oughta wear a badge."

"That's what I been tellin' him," broke in the little man. "How's people gonna know who not to shoot when they ain't no 'dentifyin' marks to see. I 'vised him to fasten it to the end of a pole. Folks what shoots sheriffs allus shoots at the badge and he'd be safe that way—if the pole was long enough."

"Will you shut yore mouth and keep still!" growled the sheriff. "I don't see what the hell I ever made you a dep'ty for, anyhow. All yore good for is to talk smart and eat often.

"What you want?" he demanded of Rance.

Hatfield handed him a letter from Captain Morton. The sheriff read it with numerous grunts and passed it to his deputy.

"You've come to a helluva place," he rumbled. "If it ain't one damn thing it's five or six. Ev'thin' was fine in Tonto county until that damn gold strike last year. Now this town's 'bout ten times bigger'n it was and all the hellions what oughta been hung and ain't is heah. The Gandara boys usta get rambunctious now and then but they waren't hard to handle 'fore things got to boomin'. Now they're on the prod all the time."

"Wheah's the town marshal?" asked Rance. The sheriff swore in disgust.

"Drunk, I s'pose. He's allus drunk, or gettin' that way, or gettin' over it. Gamblers and saloon-keepers got him 'lected. He's 'bout as much help to me as that damn dep'ty over theah."

"Name's Turner—Tumbleweed Turner," chuckled the deputy. "Don't mind Johnny, Ranger, he's got indigestion, and warts under the seat of his pants, but he's harmless."

Rance left the office with the sheriff's promise to cooperate to the best of his ability.

"Honest and dumb," was Rance's verdict. "That dep'ty's got brains. Grins and talks funny to cover up what he thinks. Them twinklin' eyes of his give me a goin'-over that didn't miss a thing."

5

If Coffin had been tumultuous under the afternoon sun, it was trebly so now that the purple shadows were leaping down from the fanged walls of The Black Hell. The daylight rumble was rising to a wild roar. Men who had just been having a drink or two were now getting grandly drunk. The roulette wheels were spinning at a mad clip. The trickle of gold across the bars had swollen to a rushing stream. The dance-halls were swirls of color.

Rance sauntered from one place of amusement to another. There was a definite object in his apparent aimless wandering. He was searching for a man, a tall gangling man with watery blue eyes and yellow hair.

"He looks like a splinter with sheep wool stuck on top of it," Tumbleweed had said, describing "Muddy" Waters, the town marshal.

Rance wanted to talk with Waters. "He ain't wuth a damn, but he knows more 'bout the wide loopin' and drygulchin' jiggers heah than anybody else 'round," declared Sheriff Bethune. "Mebbe you can get him to say somethin'."

Midnight approached, and Rance had not found the marshal.

"Heerd him say he was goin' over to the 'Here

It Is,' " a bartender told the Ranger. "Yeah, that's the big place on Lucky Cuss Street. You can't miss it."

Rance remembered the saloon as the one in which he had witnessed the shooting that afternoon. While still some distance away he ran into Sheriff Bethune and Tumbleweed Turner.

"Heah the Gandara boys is raisin' plenty hell," said the sheriff. "They jest 'bout busted the bank at Garner's place, got all the gals drunk at the Golden Place dance-hall and then headed for the Here It Is. Peter Yuma's gang hangs out theah and if them two outfits get t'gether theah's liable to be some real trouble."

"What's Pete Yuma's gang?" Rance wanted to know.

"I'd sorta like to know the answer to that one myself," growled the Sheriff. "Pete and the two Warner boys and Dirty-shirt Jones and Polecat Perkins owns the Busted Bridle mine. They hardly ever do no work but allus have plenty of money. Coupla jiggers by the name of Saunders and Paulson dropped inter town last week and got thick as sheep dip with Pete's outfit right away. They got money, too, and ain't scared to spend it. They're pop'lar. That's the Here It Is 'crost the street; let's drop over."

The big saloon was blazing with light and booming with music. Song, or what passed for it, roared through the windows, drowning the clink of glasses, the whisper of cards and the click and thump of dancing feet.

"Looks like a big night," observed Tumbleweed. "She's—good gosh!"

A gun cracked inside the saloon. Then a regular hail-on-a-tin-roof rattle of exploding six-shooters. Yells and screams raised the slab-shingles on the roof. Furniture crashed. Shattered glassware jingled. The walls of the big building seemed to bulge with the uproar. Men and women were scooting out the front door like singed bats from the place General Sherman said war was. A gentleman in a hurry took a window, glass and sash, with him. He passed Rance and the sheriffs with part of the frame still draped around his neck.

"The Gandaras and Pete Yuma's gang!" he howled. "They're fi'tin' like mad dawgs! They done killed the marshal!"

Rance Hatfield crossed the street at a run. "C'mon!" he barked over his shoulder to the sheriff, "this ain't funny no more!"

He went through the door, hurling men aside; after him plowed the sheriff and Tumbleweed.

The room was thick with smoke, through which guns spurted flame. Men were crouched behind tables and posts blazing away at other men holed up back of the bar. Two silent figures lay on the floor near the middle of the room. A third writhed and groaned beside the wall.

Rance Hatfield's voice rang above the roar of gunfire:

"Stop it, you *loco hombres*!"

A slit-eyed man back of a post whirled, his gun barrel stabbing toward the door. Rance felt the wind of the passing bullet, heard a grunt behind him and the thud of a falling body. Then his own gun lanced flame.

The man by the post crumpled up. Rance leaped to the end of the bar, a gun in each hand.

"Get the dead wood on that other bunch, Tumbleweed," he shouted.

The men back of the bar were "caught settin'." The Ranger's guns could sweep them like a stream of water from a hose. Their hands went up.

"The Gandara boys, all six of 'em," Rance muttered. "Now—"

Three shots ripped from behind a post on the far side of the room. Crashing and jangling, the three big hanging lamps went out. Darkness like the inside of a black bull swooped down.

Rance, knowing what to expect, hurled himself sideways to the floor. Bullets stormed through the space he had just left. He heard the thud of running feet. Glass crashed. Doors banged.

"Wonder if they got Tumbleweed?" he muttered. A voice bawling from somewhere in the darkness reassured him:

"You all right, Hatfield? Fine! Wait'll I make

a light. 'Fraid they done for pore old Johnny."

By the time Tumbleweed got a light going, however, the sheriff was sitting up, wiping blood from his face and swearing. He had been neatly creased just above the left ear.

"Oh, hell," grunted Tumbleweed. "If I'da knowed they hit you in the haid I wouldn'ta worried none. Nothin' theah a bullet could hurt.

"This heah jigger won't do no more shootin', though," he added, bending over a silent figure. "Drilled plumb center."

"Uh-huh, and looks like they're gonna hafta 'lect a new marshal," said Rance Hatfield. "This is Waters, ain't it?"

"Yeah, that's pore ol' Muddy," said Tumbleweed, gazing down into the face of the dead man. "Wheahd he get hit?"

"Place a man ain't got no bus'ness gettin' hit," replied Rance, turning the body over and pointing to a gaping wound between the scrawny shoulder blades. "Looks to me like he was shot 'fore the real row started."

A voice spoke at Rance's elbow.

"Guilermo Gandara shot the marshal, feller."

Rance turned to face the speaker, a little wizened man with soft brown eyes.

"What you know 'bout it?" asked the Ranger.

"I works heah," said the little man, "waitin' on tables. I seed it all. Guilermo and Pete Yuma was arg'fyin'; had their hands on their guns. Muddy was tryin' to make peace 'tween 'em. Jest as he was turnin' 'round to face Pete, Pete pulled his gun. Guilermo pulled his jest a mite faster. Muddy jumped to grab Pete's hand jest as Guilermo shot. Bullet musta hit Muddy 'stead of Pete. Anyhow Muddy whirled 'round and tumbled down. Then ev'body started shootin' and I got up and git."

Rance glanced about. "Any one of them three fellers on the floor Pete Yuma?" he asked. The deputy shook his head.

"Guess this heah feller has 'bout got the size of it, then," said Rance. "Callate Guilermo didn't 'tend to shoot Muddy.

"But this ain't no ord'nary killin'," he added soberly. "After all, Muddy was a peace officer tryin' to do his duty, and he was killed tryin' to do it. Guilermo'll hafta come in and stand trial."

"Good gosh!" exclaimed Tumbleweed. "Him and the rest of them young hellions is headed for home now, licketty-split. Tryin' to get one of 'em and bring him back heah would be like haulin' a rattlesnake out of a hole by his tail."

"Guess yore right," agreed Rance. "S'posin' you get the sheriff's haid looked after and then see what Pete Yuma and his outfit is doin'."

"All right," nodded Tumbleweed, "what you gonna do?"

"Oh, I got a little puhsonal bus'ness to look after," said the Ranger.

Rance went to the stable where he had left his

horse. *El Rey* was glad to see him and said so in horse language. Rance took time to clean his guns before he saddled up.

"You take the trail what Lucky Cuss Street runs inter and foller it nawth to wheah it branches," a sleepy hostler told him in reply to a question. "Take the branch to the left, the one what runs through Blue Rock canyon. Silver Valley is jest the other side. That's the Cross-G spread."

Dawn was breaking when Rance entered Blue Rock canyon. Silver Valley was glorious with morning when he pulled up at the northern mouth of the gloomy gorge and sat gazing at the big white *casa* set in its grove of shimmering cottonweeds.

"So that's the Gandara *hacienda*," he mused. "A fine lookin' dugout, all right. Well, heah goes."

Straight to the wide-spreading veranda he rode. *El Rey* was trained to stand and Rance left him with hanging reins.

The big front door stood open. Rance entered without knocking, walked down a broad hall and stopped before a door back of which he could hear voices. He pushed the door open and stepped into a lofty dining room.

Six men were seated at the table, eating breakfast. They stared in astonishment at the tall Ranger framed in the opening.

"Which of you fellers is Guilermo Gandara?" asked Rance.

The tallest and darkest of the men rose to his feet, eyes questioning.

"I'm Guilermo," he said. "Why?"

Rance spoke quietly, choosing his words:

"Gandara, you killed a man in Coffin this mawnin'. From what I can find out it was a sorta accidental killin'; but the man was a peace officer and yore goin' back to Coffin with me to stand trial."

Guilermo Gandara's jaw sagged, his eyes widened. He seemed incapable of speech.

"Y-you say I'm goin' back to Coffin with you?" he finally managed to stutter.

"That's what I said. You ready to ride?"

A rush of hot blood darkened Guilermo's face still more. His eyes switched from Rance to his brothers. "Boys, you heah that? He's gonna *take* me to Coffin! Well if this don't beat—"

He whirled back to the Ranger, hands sweeping down. Gripping the butts of his pearl-handled guns, he froze motionless.

Rance Hatfield's Colts had slid from their sheaths in a blur of movement too swift for the eye to follow. The black muzzles, steady as rocks, yawned toward the table. The Ranger's voice, hard and cold, bit at Guilermo:

"Yore goin' to Coffin with me, ridin' or under a blanket! Take yore choice!"

The men at the table sat tense. Guilermo still stood with whitening fingers gripping his guns. The eyes of all six were brightening, narrowing. Rance read the signals right. He had seen that chill litter birthing in the eyes of men before. Death was twirling his rope over the room.

A door on the far side of the table opened and a man entered—a strikingly handsome old man with snowy hair and vividly blue eyes. He halted on the threshold, a look of utter amazement on his face.

"What the hell's goin' on heah?" he demanded.

One of the Gandara twins answered him.

"Pappy, this feller says he's gonna take Guilermo to Coffin to stand trial for a killin'."

The old man's gaze centered on Rance.

"Who the devil are you?" he barked.

"I represent the Territory of Arizona," Rance told him, his eyes never leaving Guilermo. "I'm a Ranger and I'm arrestin' yore son for killin' Marshal Waters at Coffin. I don't think they'll anythin' much come of it, but he's gotta go to Coffin and stand trial."

The old man's face changed. He turned to Guilermo.

"I told you you was gonna get in real trouble some day with yore hell raisin'," he said. "You go ahead with this officer and don't arg'fy. I'll get to town this aft'noon and straighten this mess up. Get goin', now."

Guilermo's hands dropped from his guns. "All right, pappy," he nodded. "What you say goes."

"I'd like to change my clothes and shave 'fore I ride," he said to Rance. "You can come and watch me while I do it."

Rance glanced at the proud, handsome face, and holstered his guns.

"It ain't necessary for me to go 'long, I guess," he said. "I'll be waitin' outside, with my hoss."

A subtle change evidenced in the attitude of the Gandara boys. Much of the hostility faded from their eyes. They relaxed.

"You better have some breakfast, feller," said one as Rance turned to the door.

"Thanks," said the Ranger, "but I ain't hungry. I'll wait outside."

He sat down on the edge of the veranda and rolled a cigarette.

"Real folks livin' heah," he told the black.

For several minutes he smoked thoughtfully. He turned at the sound of a step, the cigarette dropped from his fingers and he stood up, eyes staring.

A girl had stepped out onto the veranda, a small girl with big black eyes, dark curly hair and a sweet red mouth. She was as astonished as the Ranger.

"Howdy, Ma'am," said Rance. "I didn't get a chanct to thank you right last time, so I'm doin' it now."

"Where did you come from? W-what are you doing here?" she asked.

"I'm waitin' for a feller," Rance replied to the second question, ignoring the first. "You live heah?"

She did not answer. Her gaze had left the Ranger and was fixed on *El Rey*. Once again Rance saw the color drain from her cheeks.

"That horse—" the words were little more than a whisper—"where did you get it?"

"I traded with a feller for him," Rance replied. "I got the best of the trade."

"Traded for him," repeated the girl dazedly. "Why—why—"

Hoofs clattered. Guilermo Gandara rode around a corner of the house.

"All right, feller, I'm ready," he told Rance. "Hello, Gypsy," he greeted the girl, "how's tricks?"

Without waiting for a reply he trotted down the drive, leaving Rance to follow at his convenience.

Rance flipped the reins over *El Rey*'s neck and mounted. He smiled down at the girl.

"*Adios, Senorita*," he said. "Glad you didn't have a quirt with you this mawnin'."

Color rushed back to her cheeks. Rance raised his wide hat, nodded and rode away, leaving her staring after him.

6

"Feller, you sho' have qualified to ketch rattlesnakes by the tail," said Tumbleweed Turner that night. "No wonder the Rangers is makin' a name for themselves all over the Territory, if that's a sample of the things they do. You sho' started this heah *pueblo* buzzin'.

"Co'hse it was plumb sartain from the beginnin' the coroner's jury would turn Guilermo loose," he went on, "but gettin' him 'fore the jury was what counted. He didn't seem to hold no hard feelin's 'gainst you. Who-all didja see up to their place?"

"Guilermo's pappy, his brothers and his sister," Rance replied.

"Sister? Guilermo ain't got no sister."

"Thasso? Well, theah was a mighty purty black-haired gal theah when I left."

"Oh," said Tumbleweed in an understanding voice, "you musta run inter Gypsy Carvel. She ain't them boys' sister—she's their cousin. Old Alfredo, their pappy, had a sister. She married Jim Carvel—died when the gal was born, I b'lieve. Jim got killed last yeah, I fergit jest how. She's lived with the Gandaras 'most her life."

For an instant Rance Hatfield stared with dilated eyes. Then he quickly turned away, so that the deputy might not see his whitening face.

"Jim Carvel!" he whispered through stiff lips. "Jim Carvel her father. God! if that ain't hell! What goes over the devil's back sho' comes home under his breast!"

He lay a long time before going to sleep that night, staring at the ceiling with somber eyes.

"Hell, how could I tell her!" he growled. "She wouldn't believe it nohow. Don't guess nobody would, fer that matter. Funny, ain't it, how a lie comes home to roost? Even a good lie—that is if theah ever is any sich thing as a good lie. When I told that one I thought it was plumb good, but now I ain't so sho', I ain't so sho'!"

His mind went back to the scene in the little Carvel ranch-house more than a year before. The house had been cold and silent when Rance rode up to serve the warrant on Jim Carvel. Inside he found a dying man with a gun lying beside him. Jim Carvel had shot himself.

"Don't know why I did it," Carvel mumbled. "Now I wish I hadn't. When I saw you ridin' up I figgered—'Hell, what's the use! They'll make me stretch rope for killin' Hoskins, even if he did have it comin' to him and I shot in self defense.' Yeah, Ranger, I sho' wish I hadn't done it. It'll jest about kill my kid—she's livin' with her uncle right now. Carvel folks has allus had guts—guess I'm the fust one to show yaller. Sorry—"

Touched by the dying man's story, Rance had

done an impulsive thing. In his official report concerning Jim Carvel he had written—*"Killed while resisting arrest!"*

Rance had always felt justified in that white lie. But now—

"Oh, hell!" he growled and went to sleep.

7

Rance began to ride much in the vicinity of Silver Valley, but he did not visit the Cross-G ranch-house. Not due to any unfriendliness shown him by the Gandaras, however. Several times he had met one or more of the boys in town. They had appeared to hold no animosity. Old Alfredo, on the single occasion he had encountered the ranch owner in Coffin, had spoken pleasantly.

"Fine old jigger, that," Rance had confided to *El Rey*, "but he 'pears like he's got trouble on his mind. Sorta sad and worried lookin' all the time."

From the rugged slopes of *El Infierno Negro* to the west, the Cross-G ranch-house could be seen. Rance spent a great deal of time on those slopes, where he could see and not be seen.

"If the hunch I'm follerin' is a good one, sooner or later she's gonna ride south," he told the black horse, "and when she does, why—we're headin' south, too."

Late one afternoon of golden sunlight dripping down a sky like a veil of bluebirds' wings his patience was rewarded. Earlier in the day the Gandara boys had ridden off toward Coffin. Old Alfredo had departed in the direction of his great north range. Then, just as the western peaks were ringed about with saffron flame, Rance saw a trim little figure ride away toward the purple mountains of the south. Even at that distance he could make out a blanket roll behind the saddle and the slim lines of a rifle in the saddle boot.

Rance spoke to *El Rey*, and the big black nimble-footed down the rocky slope.

For some time Rance rode at a fast gallop; then, knowing he was closing the distance between him and the girl, he reined in somewhat. From a hilltop he caught sight of her, a dot on the white trail ahead.

"Stretch yore legs a little more, hoss," he ordered. "Gonna come night 'fore long and we don't want her to give us the slip."

Soon the trail swerved slightly to the west and Rance felt easier. This was the Canyon Trail that wound through steeply walled gorges for many miles.

"Ain't but one way for her to go now," he nodded with satisfaction. "All hole-in-the-wall travellin' till you cross the line, and for a long time after."

He nodded his satisfaction again when he reached the barbed-wire fence that marked the line and found the strands had been cut and roughly joined again.

"Right on the trail," he grunted. "Now we gotta close up a bit and take our chances."

It was a moonless night of a myriad stars burning golden in the black robe of the sky.

Sounds travelled far in the silence and Rance pulled up from time to time and listened intently for the click of hoofs.

Finally he heard them, fainting away into the distance. He rode swiftly for a little while, pulled up again, and again caught the distant clicking—nearer this time.

"If she happens to stop and hear us, and gets that rifle to workin'—well, theah'll be one *good* Ranger 'round heah, 'cordin' to her way of thinkin'," he muttered. "Hoss, step light and easy!"

The golden stars began paling to silver. A wan something, like the shadow of an unborn dream, fled across the sky. It was the first breath of the coming dawn. Rance lounged wearily in the saddle, peering ahead with eyes that ached from constant strain. *El Rey* snorted disgustedly and quickened his pace. The Ranger pulled him to a halt on a hilltop and sat gazing into a great pool of shadows far below.

Coppery spears of light shot up from the east, caromed off the sky's curve and stabbed into the shadow-pool. It fled into the nothingness and Rance saw a small, lonely figure riding wearily up a distant slope. He waited until it had vanished over the crest, then he urged *El Rey* to a fast gallop.

The huge black thundered down the trail, flitted across the hollow and toiled up the opposite rise.

Again Rance halted him on the hilltop. Ahead wound the trail, a ribbon of dusty silver, deserted.

Rance swore in exasperation and fell to searching the flanking hills with a glance that missed nothing. His eyes brightened as they centered on a narrow, almost imperceptible gap only a few hundred yards down the slope from where he sat.

"That's the only place she coulda sidetracked to, hoss," he said, twitching the bridle.

A faint track ran through the gorge, with overhanging cliffs shouldering it on either side. Rance rode cautiously: the girl could not be far ahead. The gorge began to widen and his caution increased.

"Here's wheah we take to the hills, feller," he decided, turning the black to the right.

El Rey picked his way daintily between rocks and tree trunks. He avoided patches of thorny mesquite and dense manzanita thickets. Rance suddenly sniffed, and swallowed hungrily.

"Coffee bilin' somewheah clost, sho' as hell," he muttered. "Easy, hoss! Now what d'you know 'bout that?"

The downhill growth had abruptly thinned out. Rance could see into a narrow valley, grass grown and wooded. Clustered under the widely spaced trees of a grove were a score or more of roughly built huts. Before the largest of these stood a tired horse. Beside the horse a girl and a golden-haired man conversed earnestly.

The girl appeared to be urging the man to some course of which he disapproved. He shook his head repeatedly, shrugged his shoulders and gestured. Finally he patted her on the shoulder and turned toward the cabin. She followed him in and the door closed behind them. Rance sat motionless for a long time, but they did not reappear. He spoke to the horse and rode slowly up the slope.

All through the long day Rance lay concealed on the hillside, watching men come and go in the valley.

Once a row of some kind broke out and there was much shouting and cursing, in the midst of which the golden-haired man appeared in the doorway of his cabin. Rance saw the swift gleam of a thrown knife. There was a scream followed by a tense silence. The golden-haired man turned back into the cabin, closing the door behind him.

"Cavorca, yore a fangin' sidewinder," Rance muttered as he watched two men carry a limp form into another cabin, "but you sho' know how to handle them hellions what ride for you."

Rance saw nothing of the girl during the day. Cavorca appeared once or twice for a brief period, apparently receiving reports from men who had ridden in, and giving orders. Toward evening Rance slipped up the hill to where he had hobbled *El Rey*, to see that the black horse was getting his quota of grass and could reach the little stream of water that trickled down the rocks. He dozed a little as the air grew cooler.

Just as dusk was falling the girl appeared. A man brought her horse to the cabin door. Manuel Cavorca stood beside the saddle and she seemed to make a last appeal. He shook his head and she rode down the valley, her slim shoulders drooping despondently.

"That sidewinder wouldn't do anythin' decent for his own mother, I bet," growled the watching Ranger. "Wonder what she wanted of him, anyhow?

"I know damn well it waren't anythin' but somethin' he'd oughta do!" he added in the tone of a man arguing with himself.

Darkness fell, and still Rance Hatfield lay watching the lights now gleaming in the valley. He munched cold food taken from his saddlebags and tried to find soft spots in the rocks.

One by one the lights winged out, except for a single glow in the cabin of Manuel Cavorca. Rance waited another hour and rose to his feet, loosening his guns in their sheaths.

Silently he drifted down the slope. He weaved between the dark cabins, reached the one occupied by Cavorca and hesitated an instant. He hated to make a noise, but he dared not risk fooling with the latch. He lunged with a big shoulder, the door flew open and he leaped into the room.

Manuel Cavorca sat at a table, the light of an oil lamp striking bronze glints in his yellow hair and deepening the blue of his eyes. He started up as Rance confronted him, then sank back under the threat of the Ranger's gun. Recognition tensed his mouth.

"So!" he purred in his silvery voice. "My Ranger friend, eh! And what do you here, *amigo*, in Mexico?"

"I've come for you, Cavorca," said Rance quietly.

"This is not Arizona. You have no authority here."

"Yeah, but I have," drawled the Ranger, "plenty. Right heah!" He gestured with the big gun.

"One shout from me and my men will tear you to pieces," said Cavorca.

"One little cheep from you and they won't find anythin' but pieces of you when they get heah," Rance countered. "Stand up and face the wall."

Death was looking out from the Ranger's gray eyes. Manuel Cavorca read that bleak stare aright and did not hesitate. Rance took a rope that hung from a wall peg, bound him securely and slipped a gag into his mouth. He laid the outlaw's pearl-handled guns on the table beside a knife he took from a sheath at the back of his neck. Then he raised the trussed up form to his shoulder and left the cabin.

During the day Rance had noted the position of a lean-to stable where several horses were stalled. He laid Cavorca beside the trail at the mouth of the gorge and slipped back to the stable. He soothed a horse with voice and hand, cinched a saddle onto its back, slipped a bit between its jaws and led it to where he had left Cavorca, its hoofs making little or no sound on the grass. Leaving the cayuse tied to a tree, he went after *El Rey*.

With Cavorca's feet bound securely to the stirrups he rode away from the silent valley. Outside the gorge he removed the gag and untied the outlaw's hands.

"Don't see no sense in makin' you any more uncomfortable than nec'sary," he explained. "All right, keep ahead of me."

Daylight found them not far from the border, where the trail swept in a wide curve around a great hollow. Neither Rance nor his prisoner saw, at the edge of the growth far ahead, where the trail straightened out again, a weary little figure leading a badly lamed horse.

Across the curve the click of hoofs drifted to the girl's ears. She glanced over her shoulder, whirled and stood staring in astonished dismay. A low cry seeped past the little hand clenched against her red lips. For a moment she stood stricken, then she flashed into action.

Urging the crippled horse into the growth, she tied him to a branch. Overlooking the trail was a tall, sloping rock. She scrambled to the top of this, crouched behind a ledge and rested her rifle in a shallow crack.

On came the clicking hoofs. Two horses ambled around the bend.

"*Alto ahi! Hands up!*"

Rance "halted where he was." His hands tensed, then slowly rose to a level with his shoulders. There was no sense arguing with that black rifle muzzle looking him between the eyes. Cavorca halted also.

"All right," said the Ranger, "we done halted. What next you want?"

"You ride ahead," replied the voice. "Keep your hands up! Manuel Cavorca, pull your horse aside."

Rance touched *El Rey* with his knees and the black moved slowly forward. Cavorca grinned exultantly into the Ranger's face.

Rance did not answer.

"Halt!" called the voice before he had gone a dozen paces. Then it rose in a scream of breaking nerves:

"Ride, Manuel, ride. Back into Mexico! No! No! Don't you touch him! I'll shoot *you* if you do!"

Rance glanced over his shoulder and saw Cavorca, his face convulsed with hatred. There was a knife in his hand. Where it had been concealed Rance had no idea.

"I mean it, Manuel!" screamed the hidden voice.

Cavorca hissed a curse and swung his horse around. Heedless of his feet bound to the stirrups, he urged the animal to a gallop. Rance sat motionless, his hands still raised. The drum of hoofs droned to a whisper, died away. From the rock beside the trail sounded a scuffle and scramble. Rance lowered his hands, turned *El Rey* and sat waiting.

Curly head held high, eyes defiant, Gypsy Carvel stepped into view, the rifle swinging loosely under her arm.

"All right," she said. "I'm ready. You can take me to jail for helping your prisoner to escape."

Rance regarded her somberly for a moment. Then a grin quirked his lips and set little lights to dancing in his gray eyes.

"Guess we're a *coupla* law breakers, ma'am," he said. "You see, we're still in Mexico, and I ain't got a bit of authority in Mexico. I was jest doin' a little job of wide loopin' on that jigger."

"Oh!" said the girl.

The smile left the Ranger's face. "But it's sho' got me puzzled why you'd help a murderin' sidewinder like that to get loose," he added.

Her head went up again. "He's no worse than people who murder with the law protecting them!"

Rance opened his lips to reply, and bit back the words unspoken; they would be but wasted effort, he decided.

"Wheah's yore hoss?" he said instead.

Twilight was falling when they reached Silver Valley, *El Rey* carrying double, the girl's horse loping along behind.

"*Adios*, until our next fight," Rance nodded as she slipped to the ground.

"Wait," she said. "You must be very hungry, and it is a long ride to Coffin."

"Much 'bliged, ma'am," he answered, turning *El Rey*'s head, "but I don't hanker to eat with folks what figger me a paid killer."

Gypsy Carvel's soft lips trebled slightly and there was a dejected droop to her dark head as she walked up the drive to the big white *casa*.

8

Rance found Coffin roaring as never before. The rickety board walks were thronged with laughing, singing, shouting men, most of them grandly drunk. Horsemen galloped up and down the streets, yelling and shooting holes in the sky. Even the fights had taken on a joyous note; men actually seemed to get pleasure out of being knocked down! The smell of whiskey, the glitter of gold and the haze of powder smoke rose like a swamp miasma to blot out the stars.

The Ranger entered a saloon to find out what it was all about. A perfect stranger seized his hand and pump-handled it with vast enthusiasm. A girl he had never seen before threw her arms around his neck.

Rance freed his hand from the whooping miner's grip and touseled the girl's hair.

"What the blazes is going on?" he demanded.

"Another strike!" howled the miner. "The biggest ever! Have a drink on me!"

"They hit it rich in Silver Valley, yesterday—way up to the northern end clost to *El Infierno Negro*," a bartender explained. "The hull damn town's gone crazy!"

Rance looked grave. "On the Cross-G spread?"

"Yeah," said the drink juggler. "Old Alfredo and his boys rode in yest'day and filed claims and then 'vited ev'body to head up theah and stake out workin's. Real people, them Gandaras!"

"They sho' are," agreed Rance.

"You'll find 'em down at the Here It Is," said the bartender. "They're celebratin'."

Rance found the Gandara boys in the big saloon, buying rounds of drinks for the house. They welcomed him boisterously.

"Ain't no use of ever 'restin' me any more, Ranger," chuckled Guilermo. "T'morrer I'm gonna buy me the jail and the co'ht house!"

Old Alfredo was seated at a table, grinning at the antics of his sons. He nodded to Rance to join him.

"Sho' glad to heah of yore good luck, suh," Rance congratulated him.

"Yeah, she come in handy," Alfredo admitted. "Things ain't been so good in the cow bus'ness lately, what with them two dry yeahs and the big blizzard last winter. We can use a little extra money right now. We been doin' a little quiet perspectin' for quite a while. I figgered that them Dry Bone Coulee deposits had oughta crop up again on our side the hills, and I figgered it right. I took up claims for me and the boys, and one for my niece. Theah's another one I'm tryin' to hang onto for my youngest kid—the one what went away—but I'm scairt I won't be able to, him not bein' heah to register it. Makes me feel bad, too."

Rance nodded sympathetically. "You ain't got no idea wheah he is, then?"

Old Alfredo shook his head. "Nope. Last heerd tell of him he was somewheah in Mexico. He was a wild younker and got inter some bad shootin' scrapes and lit out coupla yeahs ago.

"Funny thing," the ranch owner went on, "he was the only one of the boys what looked like his maw. The rest of the boys sorta take after me—big and dark—guess the Spanish blood hangs on purty strong. She had blue eyes and yaller hair and waren't very big. I'd hoped the kid would marry Gypsy Carvel, his cousin, but they didn't seem to take to each other that way. More of a brother and sister feelin', but they sho' thought a heap of each other. I sometimes think Gypsy knows wheah he is and won't tell."

Rance sat thoughtful for some minutes. He had been touched by the old man's steadfast affection for his scapegrace son and his desire to provide for his future.

"Mr. Gandara," he offered at length, "I got a little suggestion to make—mebbe it'll sound good to you."

Old Alfredo looked interested. "Uh-huh?"

"S'posin'," said Rance, a trifle diffidently, "you let me file that claim in my name. Fust, I'll deed it over to yore son—that's permitted, you know—and when he shows up it'll be theah ready for him. You can hire somebody to do the assay work."

Old Alfredo beamed. "Now that's mighty fine of you!" he exclaimed. "Mighty fine. I accept that offer and I'm sho' much obliged. We'll drop over to Benson's office and fix up the papers, if yore 'greeable. And while yore at it, why don't you file a claim for yoreself. I've a notion theah's still some valyble ledges left."

Rance smiled, but shook his head. "I ain't a miner," he said. "I'm a Ranger, and I still owns a little int'rest in a cow factory. Guess I got too much hoss flesh and saddle leather and grass rope in my blood to ever be keen for much of anythin' else."

Rance heard more news the next day—news of a disquieting nature.

"It's Pete Yuma," Tumbleweed Turner told the Ranger. "Him and Dirty Shirt is makin' big talk. They blame you for the Warner boys bein' killed and they don't feel so happy 'bout what happened to Saunders and Paulson. Pete says he's gonna run you outa town or kill you; been spoutin' it 'round ev'wheah."

"Bit talk don't us'ally mean much," commented Rance.

Tumbleweed's face was earnest; there was no twinkle in his eyes now.

"Don't be too sho'," he warned. "Pete is bad, even though he has got a big mouth. He's a killer and he shoots fast and straight, pref'ably in the back. Dirty Shirt's the one to look out for, though. That half-breed's got what I don't believe Pete has when it comes to a show-down; Dirty Shirt's got guts."

Rance pondered the warning and did not discount it. In saloons and dance-halls as the day wore on he heard more about Yuma's threats. He also received friendly warnings and advice. All of which caused his gray eyes to harden and his lean jaw to set a little tighter. Pete Yuma was shrewdly developing a situation that would force the Ranger to take action or lose prestige, and a peace officer of the Southwest who lost prestige usually lost his life very soon after. Rance went looking for Pete Yuma, and received another warning.

"Keep away from the 'Bottoms Up', Ranger," whispered a bartender as he poured a drink. "Pete Yuma and Dirty Shirt is theah, waitin' for you to walk in the door. They been guzzlin' all day long and Dirty Shirt's smokin' *marihuana*."

Rance's eyes narrowed still more on receiving that last bit of information. *Marihuana*, a drug derived from a plant allied to *cannibus indica*, does plenty to the average white man; but it all too often changes the Indian to a merciless killer. Dirty Shirt was half Indian.

The Bottoms Up was a small saloon of evil reputation that squatted where the more pretentious buildings of Lucky Cuss Street dwindled dejectedly to shacks and dirty tents.

Rance nodded his thanks to the friendly barkeep, paid for his drink and walked slowly down Lucky Cuss Street. As he passed the last shop and entered the shack town, he noticed a rat-faced little man scurrying along in front of him. He grinned faintly as the man glanced shiftily over his shoulder and vanished between a couple of shacks.

"Jigger hustlin' 'long to tell Pete I'm headed this way," chuckled the Ranger as he turned into an alley.

Rance followed the alley for a short distance and then turned at right angles, taking a course that would put him past the back door of the Bottoms Up.

The door stood slightly ajar. Rance pushed it a bit farther open and peeped into the dingy room. The setting that met his eyes was tableau-like.

Several men, all looking one way, were ranged along the walls. The bartender, tense and alert, stood against the back bar, a sawed-off shotgun conveniently within reach. Dirty Shirt Jones stood in front of the bar, peering with muddy eyes. Pete Yuma lounged against a table, right hand caressing the black butt of his pistol. The attention of all was fixed on the front door. A grin quirked Rance Hatfield's lips but his eyes remained cold.

"Howdy, Pete!"

Pete Yuma jumped a foot, clutching convulsively at his gun. Dirty Shirt tensed rigid.

"Oh, my Gawd!" whimpered the bartender.

Turning they saw Rance Hatfield standing just inside the back door, hands on his hips, eyes glinting in the shadow of his wide hat. For a long moment there was utter silence. Then Rance walked forward until he was within three feet of Pete Yuma.

"Heah'd tell you was lookin' for me, Pete," he drawled easily.

Yuma tried to moisten his dry lips with a tongue that felt like leather.

"I—I—" he began haltingly.

"I'm heah," Rance interrupted him coldly. "Speak yore piece."

Yuma glanced about desperately. The men along the wall avoided his gaze. The bartender had moved away from the shotgun and was busily polishing a glass. Dirty Shirt's thick lips curled in a sneer.

"What the hell would I wanta see you for?" Yuma mumbled querulously.

"Thought you might have a little notion 'bout killin' me, p'haps," the Ranger said. "Well, get goin'!"

Yuma's shifty eyes refused to meet the bleak gray gaze that never left his face. His fingers curled away from the pistol butt.

Rance Hatfield suddenly reached out a long arm. He gripped the gunman by the collar, shook him till his teeth rattled.

"You little rattler!" he rasped, "you go spittin' out any more pizen 'bout me 'round heah and I'll tie you inter a bow-knot and hang you around yore own neck! Now git!"

He whirled Yuma around and hurled him half way to the door.

With a strangled scream Dirty Shirt leaped, steel glittering in his hand. Rance ducked under the knife, caught the half-breed's wrist and hurled him over his shoulder. Dirty hit the floor with a crash, writhed and lay groaning. Rance whipped his left-hand six from its holster and covered Yuma, whose gun was coming.

"Pete," he told the paralyzed outlaw, "yore leavin' town in jest three hours. If you ain't gone by then I'm comin' lookin' for you, and not with no opry glass, either. Git!"

Yuma slunk through the door. Rance jerked Dirty Shirt to his feet and shoved him, stumbling and muttering, out of the saloon and up the street to the squat, solidly built little jail.

"Lock this fangin' sidewinder up till I decides what to do with him," he told Tumbleweed Turner, who acted as turnkey.

After the deputy had departed on some business of his own, Rance glanced at his watch and sat down in the little room that served as the jail office. With his feet propped comfortably on the table he smoked numerous cigarettes, looking at his watch from time to time. As the shadows lengthened he lighted the single wall lamp and resumed his seat, his lean profile etched by the yellow flame. Finally he looked at his watch for the last time and slipped it back into its pocket.

"Time's up, Pete," he drawled, half-aloud. "Now I'll just go see if—"

Cr-r-rash!

The building rocked to a terrific explosion. The heavy cell door flew off its hinges, smashed into the table and sent table, chair and Ranger to the floor in a splintering heap. Both barrels of a shotgun roared outside the window and blew what was left of the glass to bits.

Rance heard the buckshot howl over his head and slam into the wall. He pawed from under the wrecked furniture and leaped to his feet. There was an instant of silence, then the click of fast hoofs fading away from the jail.

Outside the building, men were running and shouting. The front door banged open.

"What the hell's goin' on?" bawled Sheriff Bethune.

"Pete Yuma jest left town," Rance told him dryly. Tumbleweed was peering amid the wreckage of the cell.

"Dirty Shirt's left, too," he grunted, "but they

ain't much left. Johnny, wonder wheah we can get a broom and a dust pan?"

Sheriff Johnny voiced profane comment. "Pete musta tried to help Dirty bust outa jail. The damn fool used enough dynamite to sink a battleship!"

9

The news of the Silver Valley gold strike spread swiftly. Miners and prospectors poured into Coffin. After them came a pestilent horde of gamblers, sharpers and "dance-hall" women. The newcomers, most of them, brought money. The prospect holes in the hills were coughing gold at a lively rate. The already feverish tempo of life in the mining town stepped up. Saloons, gambling hells and dance-halls flourished and grew arrogant. Fights and killings became more frequent. Sheriff Bethune, Tumbleweed Turner and the new town marshal, an energetic individual with a notched gun barrel, found plenty to do.

Rance Hatfield held himself aloof from minor local disturbances and concentrated on the outlaws, whose chief victims were miners bringing in dust from outlying claims. Robberies, which had become of too common occurrence to elicit much comment, began to decline. Rance, heading a posse of miners and cowboys, fought a pitched battle with a raiding band from Mexico and made quite a bit of work for the grave diggers. Several gentlemen who had thought themselves artists with the six-shooter suffered from lead poisoning. Others languished in the new jail.

"That damn Ranger with a gun," complained one, "is 'zactly my idea of hell!"

His views were accepted as authentic by others of the fraternity.

One development relative to the gold strike gave the Ranger much food for thought. Among the newcomers there was a growing resentment against the Gandara family.

"That damn outfit," said a shifty-eyed individual who dressed like a miner but spent most of his time at the gambling tables, "they hogged all the very best claims right in the beginning 'fore anybody else had a chanct. I s'gest somethin' bein' done 'bout it."

His sentiments were heartily endorsed by others of similar ilk. Older miners who endeavored to point out that the Gandaras had merely exercised the right of discovery and had been the first to spread the news of the strike were hooted down. Their argument did not appeal to newcomers who had been unable to stake paying claims.

"Theah's goin' to be trouble sho' as hell," an old miner confided to Rance. "That gang is organizin' and they'll start somethin' sooner or later. I done seen claim jumpin's befo' and they ain't nice things to look at."

"Anybody tryin' to jump the Gandaras' claims is apt to meet with a sorta warm reception," the Ranger said.

"Uh-huh," said the other, "but thirty or forty

to seven is purty big odds, and once the gang gits sot in them diggin's they can haul out all kinda things like blind leads and old monuments showin' prior discov'ry to prove they got the right of it. Better keep yore eyes open, Ranger."

Rance "kept them open," and he didn't like the looks of what he saw.

"We gotta get some *vigilantes* organized," he told Johnny Bethune, "fellers we can depend on when we need 'em. Hell's gonna bust loose or I'm a sheepherder."

It broke a few nights later, in the Here It Is saloon. A friend of Tumbleweed Turner's came to the sheriff's office, where Tumbleweed and Rance Hatfield were squabbling amicably over a game of seven-up.

"Guilermo Gandara is in town," said the visitor. "He's drinkin' purty heavy and been doin' quite a bit of talkin'. He met that jigger, Trainor, who's been responsible for most of the ruckus stirred up 'gainst the Gandaras. Guilermo laid down the law to him purty plain. Trainor took water, but he's been gettin' his friends t'gether and I figger they're aimin' to jump Guilermo."

Rance riffled the cards together and placed the deck in a drawer.

"Guess we'd better mosey down and look things over a bit," he told Tumbleweed.

They got word of Guilermo but could not locate him directly. He was not in the Here It Is, which they investigated first, nor in any of the other Lucky Cuss Street places. They had no better luck in the side streets. Their quarry seemed always just ahead of them.

"Let's go back to the Here It Is and wait on him," suggested Tumbleweed at last.

The Here It Is was booming as they approached. Fiddles whined, guitars strummed loudly. French heels clicked and heavy boots thumped on the dance floor. Glasses clinked. Roulette wheels whirred. Song roared through the windows.

Then, just as Rance and the deputy reached the swinging doors, the uproar dwindled away in ragged fringes of sound. A woman screamed, once, a scream sliced off by the knife of fear. Rance leaped into the room.

Standing with his back to the bar was Guilermo Gandara, his black eyes gleaming, a gun in his hand. Spread out fanwise, facing him, were six men, Ike Trainor, the leader of the claim-jumping advocates, slightly in front. Trainor was arguing with Guilermo, who watched him intently.

There was a flash at the inner edge of the "fan," a gun roared and Guilermo slewed sideways, pulling trigger as he went down. The man who had shot him doubled up with a scream.

Instantly the saloon seemed to explode with the roar of six-shooters. Rance Hatfield, firing with both hands, leaped in front of Guilermo's prostrate form. Tumbleweed Turner's bullets raked the curve of the "fan." Answering shots smashed the mirrors and knocked the glass from the door. Ike Trainor dived through a window and escaped, leaving three of his men on the floor and two with their hands in the air.

Guilermo drew himself up against the bar and pressed reddening fingers to his left arm.

"Not killed, eh?" grunted Hatfield.

"Nope, jest a hole through the muscle," panted Guilermo. "Hurts like hell but ain't serious. Thanks, Ranger. 'Nother minute and they'da put so many holes in me I'da leaked all my vittles out and starved to death."

"You get fixed up and go home," Rance told him. "This town ain't healthy for you right now."

Guilermo rode out of town shortly afterward. Rance Hatfield went to bed. Tumbleweed Turner was pounding on his door before sun-up.

"She's busted right this time, feller," chattered the little deputy. "Trainor and a bunch left town for Silver Valley durin' the night. They left word they was gonna lynch Guilermo for killin' that jigger, but what they're really aimin' for is to jump the Gandara claims."

"Get the *vigilantes* t'gether," Rance ordered, hurrying into his clothes.

Tumbleweed paused at the door.

"I heahd the Gandaras are guardin' their claims," he said. "Mebbe them jiggers will get a reception they ain't figgerin' on."

The sun was high in the sky when the posse reached Silver Valley, with two hours of hard riding ahead of them before they could hope to come to the site of the claims.

"I'm ridin' ahaid to see what's goin' on," Rance told Sheriff Bethune.

All morning *El Rey* had been chafing at being held back to the slower pace of the other horses. Now, when Rance gave him his head, he snorted joyously, slugged at the bit and stretched his long legs. Soon the posse was but a dust cloud far behind.

An hour passed, part of another. To the Ranger's ears came a faint popping, as of crisply burning sticks. His eyes narrowed, he leaned forward and spoke to the horse. *El Rey* blew foam from his spreading nostrils and lengthened his stride. The popping became the spiteful crack of revolvers, with now and then the deeper voices of rifles.

"The boys ain't been pried loose yet," muttered the Ranger.

The trees that sprinkled the valley began to thin. They spaced out to solitary sentinels and Rance saw the raw gashes on a distant hillside that marked the claims. From behind mounds of earth and heaps of stone flickered little jets of flame, palely golden in the sunlight. Whirls and wisps of blue smoke drifted up before the reports reached his ears. From the valley below, wherever a tree or a ledge or a clump of stones afforded shelter, answering smoke and flames spouted.

"A reg'lar young war!" growled the Ranger, pulling *El Rey* down to an amble.

A bullet screamed over his head. Another kicked up a patch of dust a few feet to his left.

"Spotted us," he muttered. "In behind them rocks, feller, 'fore you get a hole in yore hide!"

Working up among the rocks, he reached a point where he could see and not be seen by the men in the valley. He cast anxious glances back the way he had come, straining his eyes for a glimpse of the posse.

Suddenly he stiffened, staring toward where the crags and canyons of The Black Hell loomed darkly.

"Now who the blazes is that?" he wondered.

Horsemen were pouring from a distant canyon mouth. Rance counted a score or more.

"It can't be the boys," he insisted. "Theah's too many of 'em and 'sides they never coulda got 'round that way."

On came the riders, toiling up a slope, thundering across the floor of the valley. Puffs of smoke mushroomed up from their loosely-flung ranks.

The men in the valley saw them now, and got a taste of their bullets. Flame vomited from behind the trees. Rifles and pistols drummed a thunder roll.

Rance sent *El Rey* scrambling from among the rocks. Bullets or no bullets, he was going to see what was going on!

Men were being knocked from the saddles, but sprawling figures among the trees showed that they were not walking across into Eternity by themselves. Rance Hatfield, riding swiftly toward the battle, swore an astounded oath.

In the lead of the charging horsemen were two mounted figures that he recognized. One was trim and slender, a sweetly rounded little figure swaying lithely to the movements of her horse.

"Gypsy Carvel!" gurgled Rance. "Well, I'll be—and theah's Manuel Cavorca or I'm a dogie's hind foot!"

Hatless, his golden hair shimmering in the sunlight, the outlaw, shooting with both hands, distanced his companion. Rance could see his handsome face, distorted by the killerlust, could almost feel the blaze of his blue eyes.

"That jigger's a devil got outa hell ahead of the Jedgment!" muttered the Ranger.

Suddenly the girl's horse reared high, almost unseating her. It screamed with pain, whirled and went thundering on a long diagonal toward where the valley floor fell away to a rugged gorge that flanked The Black Hell. An instant later Rance had *El Rey* pulled around and was racing in pursuit. Gypsy Carvel's horse had been shot in the mouth, the bit knocked loose, leaving her powerless to guide the frenzied animal. Fighting to control her mount, she did not notice what Rance from his vantage point of higher ground had seen.

Directly in the maddened bronk's path lay the almost perpendicular side of the gorge, its lip fringed and hidden by thick bushes.

With voice and hand Rance urged *El Rey* to a supreme effort. The black horse, pouring out his very soul in wind-like speed, swiftly closed the distance, charging down on the runaway at a slant.

Gripping the reins with his left hand, Rance leaned far to the right. *El Rey*'s black nose reached the other horse's flank, gained an inch, a straining foot. Rance leaned farther.

There was a crash of parting bushes, the wounded horse screamed an almost human scream of terror and went plunging over and over down the slope to the rocks below.

Rance Hatfield, gripping Gypsy with his right arm, clinging to the reins with his left, braced himself as *El Rey* also went over the lip. In the final split second of time he had snatched her from the saddle.

El Rey did not lose his balance. Down the slope he went, slipping and teetering, snorting as his hoofs clattered across smooth rock. He skittered magnificently down a last nearly-straight-up-and-down stretch, "sittin' on his tail," and reached the bottom, on his feet and uninjured.

Rance Hatfield looked down into the white face of the girl.

"Ma'am," he drawled softly, "guess that evens us on that snake haid!"

Rifles were still cracking. Shouts and screams drifted down to them. Rance wheeled *El Rey* and rode swiftly down the gorge until he reached a place the horse could climb.

"Where are you going?" panted the girl.

"I got a little bus'ness to 'tend to," Rance told her.

El Rey surged over the gorge lip and stood blowing. Rance glanced about with eager eyes.

The posse was storming up the valley less than a hundred yards distant. Rance raced to meet them.

"Take her!" he ordered, thrusting the girl into Sheriff Bethune's arms.

Before the astounded sheriff could protest, Rance had wheeled *El Rey* again and was riding to where all that were left of Ike Trainor's claim jumpers were holding up their hands and bawling for mercy. The mysterious riders were streaming back into the canyon whence they had just come. Last of all, astride a limping horse and far behind his men, rode Manuel Cavorca. A last gleam of golden hair and the canyon had swallowed him.

Scant minutes later, Rance Hatfield, his eyes slits of gray fire in his grim face, also vanished between the dark portals.

Without attempt at concealment, Rance urged *El Rey* on. He must overtake the outlaw before the fleeing bandits discovered his absence. He had to take the chance of an ambush.

A half-mile, a mile, between close, frowning walls. Cavorca could not be far ahead. The canyon wound and turned like a snake in a cactus patch, its beetling cliffs flinging back a maddening confusion of echoes. Rance leaned low in the saddle, wondering if his own horse was making all that racket.

Around a sharp turn, and there, scarce fifty yards ahead, was Cavorca!

Outlaw and Ranger saw each other at the same time. Cavorca's gun roared, the bullet creased *El Rey*'s flank and the black horse went momentarily insane.

Plunging and snorting, hurling himself toward the outlaw in prancing zig-zags, he made it utterly impossible for Rance to shoot with accuracy. One of his guns was empty. A wild plunge knocked the other one from his hand. Cavorca, sitting his motionless horse, fired coolly with careful aim.

The Ranger's quick mind saw but a single desperate chance, and he took it. Flinging himself sideways from the saddle, he clutched the stock of the rifle protruding from the boot as he went down. *If the rifle stuck he would be a dead man in another instant!*

His sweaty palms slipped on the smooth stock. The hammer snagged on something. The grip of one hand was torn loose. Then he was under the plunging horse, clinging to the rifle with one desperate hand.

Over he rolled, flinging the gun up, his gray eyes glancing along the sights.

The rifle roared. Cavorca, in the act of throwing down for a last shot, stiffened, rose in his stirrups and pitched from the saddle.

Rance scrambled to his feet, rifle ready; but the outlaw lay still.

"Feller," Rance told the trembling black, "you came darn neah sunfishin' yoreself outa a good boss!"

Rance walked over and took a look at Cavorca. The rifle bullet had cut a neat furrow along the side of his head.

"Jest creased. Be settin' up cussin' in another five minutes," the Ranger decided.

Cavorca cursed plenty a little later, as securely bound, he rode his limping horse out of the canyon, Rance Hatfield following behind. They met the posse, Gypsy Carvel and the Gandaras scrambling down the slope. The girl's face was paper-white, her eyes great dark pools of pain. Rance Hatfield's own face grew bleak as his gaze met hers.

"Sorry, ma'am, but I hadda do it," his lips framed the words.

"Who the hell you got theah, Ranger?" shouted Tumbleweed Turner. "What did he—"

The little deputy's voice was drowned by an anguished cry:

"My God! Manuel! My son! My son!"

Rance Hatfield's face went white as the girl's as he stared at old Alfredo Gandara.

"Yore son!" he gasped. "Manuel Cavorca, this murderin' outlaw! yore son?"

"I tried to save him," sobbed Gypsy. "I begged him not to come here; but when he heard those men were going to jump our claims he went mad with rage."

Silently the posse rode out of Silver Valley, the snarling Manuel Cavorca, Ike Trainor and the other prisoners in their midst. Rance Hatfield stared straight ahead with brooding eyes.

"I ain't blamin' you," said old Alfredo brokenly, "you were doin' yore duty; but it's hard, feller, it's hard!"

Rance turned and looked into Gypsy Carvel's eyes. Something he saw there lifted some of the shadows from his own eyes. Impulsively he held out his hand.

"Goodbye, ma'am."

She hesitated an instant, then placed her slim fingers in his grasp.

"Goodbye, Ranger."

10

"And it is the sentence of this court that you be hanged by the neck until you are dead!"

Manuel Cavorca took it standing. Not a line of his inhumanly handsome face quivered. The mocking smile that had hovered about his perfectly formed but cruel mouth during his trial did not fade. His blue eyes stared straight into the stern face of the old jurist. Nothing, it appeared, could shake the iron nerve of the bandit.

"Don't look like a greaser, does he?" whispered a spectator in the back of the courtroom.

"Ain't no Mexican," another whispered back. "American born—old Spanish stock. He—"

Crash!

A side window flew into a million splinters. The black barrel of a heavy six-gun jutted through the opening, blazing fire and smoke.

The old judge half rose in his chair, then slumped back with a groan, clutching at his shoulder with reddening fingers. Sheriff Dobson leaped to his feet, tugging at his Colt. A bullet took him squarely between the eyes. Another knocked Deputy Hank Thomas sprawling.

Men surged through the door—dark-faced men with *sombreros* pulled low. They menaced the courtroom crowd with pistols and rifles. A voice rang out:

"Manuel, to me—*pronto!*"

Cavorca went—"quickly!" He kicked the dying deputy aside, jumped over the sheriff's body and lunged for the door. A brawny cattleman leaped from the snarling confusion of the benches and tried to stop him. Cavorca weaved aside. A slim figure in the doorway, masked and *seraped*, snapped a shot past him and the ranch owner went down. Cavorca hurdled the twitching form and reached the door.

"This way," shrilled the masked voice—a woman's voice—"horses, Manuel!"

Cavorca and the masked girl vanished. The courtroom seemed to explode with the reports of six-shooters. Ranch owners and cowboys fought themselves free from the milling mob of town loafers and courtroom hangers-on and were shooting it out with the dark-faced bandits. One went down, drilled dead center. Another cursed himself through the doorway, his gun arm swinging limp. His companions, crouching low over their smoking sixes, back-stepped after him. Outside sounded a clatter of swift hoofs.

Rance Hatfield wasn't in the courtroom when sentence was pronounced. He was at a nearby restaurant surrounding a husky portion of pig's-hip-and-hen-fruit.

"I roped myself enough hell droppin' my loop

on that jigger 'thout listenin' to the jedge 'splain to him he's gotta do a dance on nothin'," Rance told himself. "I never did fancy hearin' that kinda—*sufferin' sandtoads!*"

Chair and table went over as the Ranger leaped for the door. He hurled the squalling Chinese hash slinger aside and reached the street, guns sliding from their sheaths.

Yells, screeches, the crackle of pistol shots and blue smoke boiled from the courthouse, two blocks down the street. Horses were plunging and snorting in front of the building, shadowy and distorted in the gathering dusk.

Like pips from a squeezed orange, two figures shot from the courthouse door. They flung themselves into saddles, wheeled their frantic horses and streaked it down the street.

Rance Hatfield's guns let go with a rattling crash. One of the fleeing figures was bareheaded and Rance caught the glint of hair golden as sunlight in a lily's cup.

"That sidewinder! He's loose again!" gritted the Ranger, firing as fast as he could pull trigger.

Down went Cavorca's horse, plunging and kicking. The outlaw was hurled over his head. He turned a complete handspring in the air, lit on his feet and lit running. The other fugitive pulled to a hoof-sliding halt. Cavorca left the ground like a spring, forked the bronk behind the saddle, and away went the pair!

Rance, shoving cartridges into his empty guns, saw them vanish around a turn.

Men were boiling from the courthouse. Bullets began to strike all around the Ranger. He dodged behind a post and returned the fire with interest. He emptied two saddles as quickly as they were filled; but the post wasn't thick enough he realized as a slug cut a furrow along the inside of his left arm and another grazed his right cheek.

He went across the street in a zig-zag run, paused in the scant shelter of a hitch-rack and emptied his guns after the dying thunder of hoofs.

A shouting, milling crowd filled the street. "The Ranger got two of them," somebody yelled, "and theah's another dead one inside the co'ht house."

Rance loaded his guns and walked down the street. "Cavorca got away!" a fat man squalled at him. Rance recognized the fat man as the town's mayor.

"Oh-huh, I see he did," Rance replied.

"Ye-a-ah!" raved the fat mayor, "jest goes to show what a helluva lot of use the Rangers are! Let a herd of greaser gun slingers amble 'crost the Line, shoot respectable citizens down and snake a damn murderer right outa the co'ht house. Rangers! Jest a lotta lazy pants-seat warmers usin' up the taxpayers' money! This'll settle the lot of you, though. Come the next legislature and the territory'll be shed of you!"

For a moment the utter injustice of the attack left Rance speechless. Before he had recovered, another was speaking. Rance recognized Walsh Patton, the county prosecutor. Patton was an angular, lantern-jawed individual with mean eyes and a meaner disposition. He was political boss of Cochise county and had a pull that reached all the way to Washington.

"Keepin' a eye on the Border's a Ranger job, ain't it?" demanded Patton. "That's one of the arg'ments used to get the last legislature to vote for organizin' the Rangers. Swell job yore doin'. Tomas Fuentes and his whole damn revolution army could come 'crost any time he feels like it, for all anythin' you fellers'd do to stop him."

Rance Hatfield's lips set in a grim line, choking back the angry words of reply that stormed for expression. Nothing would be gained by arguing with either Patton or Mayor Thomas. Nothing would be gained by reminding them that the help the Rangers had offered to safeguard Cavorca had been curtly refused by the county authorities. Patton and Thomas, leaders of a clan bitterly opposed to the newly formed body, The Arizona Rangers, would make the most of the convicted bandit's escape, slurring over their own culpability, using every means in their power to cause the territory in general to believe Ranger negligence was responsible. Rance quietly asked a question:

"How many got killed in the co'hthouse?"

The sheriff and his deputy were dead, Rance quickly learned. Two cowboys and the cattleman, Blanton, were badly wounded. The judge was suffering from shock and a smashed shoulder. The bandits had taken their wounded with them.

"Ain'tcha gonna get a posse t'gether and chase 'em?" the fat mayor demanded of Rance.

"Chase 'em wheah?" asked the Ranger, jerking a scornful head toward the purple mountains looming only a few miles south of the town. "Theah's Mexico, so clost you can hit it with a rock. They're acrost the Line by now, wheah we ain't got no 'thority. And don't fool yoreself, feller," he added, "theah's a young army jinin' Cavorca down theah."

The mayor indulged in a sneer, after Rance had walked away.

"Theah's the Rangers for you!" he snorted. "Ain't got the guts to get a posse t'gether and chase them fellers!"

A lanky, hard-bitten cowboy regarded him coldly.

"I rec'lects it was that theah same Ranger what caught Cavorca in the fust place, and 'tacked his whole gang and got shot up doin' it," he drawled. "Likewise it was the Ranger's gun what 'counted for two o' them three 'good' bandits layin' over theah under blankets. I figger you fellers'd do well to sing sorta small fer a while."

11

Rance had his wounded arm bandaged. Then he rode out of town, alone. He headed north.

"What them jiggers back theah don't know won't hurt 'em, and, what's a darn sight more important, it won't hurt us," he told his magnificent black stallion, *El Rey*. "I ain't so sho' but somebody theah knowed all 'bout that raid 'fore it happened. It was timed mighty fine for guesswork."

As the Ranger rode, he did some very serious thinking.

"Patton and Thomas waren't talkin' for me to hear," he growled. "They was talkin' to the crowd. They're buildin' up a case 'gainst the Rangers, and 'tween you and me, hoss, they're doin' a purty darn good job of it. No use tellin' folks they practically ordered us to stay away from their blasted town while the trial was goin' on. They'll jest keep on squallin' that it was the Rangers' job to keep that gang from sneakin' 'crost the Line. They'll spread it 'bout that if the Rangers had had their eyes open it couldn'ta happened. Thomas owns a newspaper and Patton has the ear of all the political big bugs in the territory. Hoss, theah's jest one way out—and you and me has gotta hawgtie Cavorca again!"

Out of the Ranger's desperation had been born a plan—a plan fraught with such danger and difficulty as to make its success possible through its very daring. Rance tied its loose ends together as he rode through the lovely blue dusk of the southwest. Three miles north of the town he entered a gloomy canyon.

The canyon wound and twisted in a confusing manner. When Rance finally rode out of it, under a blazing net of stars that seemed to brush the mountain tops, he was headed a trifle south of west. A little later he turned into a dim track that ran due south.

"This oughta cut 'crost their trail," he mused. "I figger they'll head straight for Paloa. That's a tough *pueblo* if theah ever was one. It's Tomaso Fuentes' town, too, and Fuentes is too big a shot for even the Diaz gov'ment to monkey with, much. Cavorca'll feel safe theah till he gets his bearin's."

A few miles farther on the track *did* cross another trail, a better and more travelled one. Rance nodded with satisfaction.

His satisfaction was even greater when he reached a sagging barbed-wire fence. Where the fence crossed the trail, the strands had been cut! Without hesitation Rance rode through the gap. He had another talk with his horse.

"Guess you know, feller, that fence marks the

Line. We're in Mexico now and the only 'thority we got heah is what we carries in our heels and holsters. Them heels of yores has got us outa more'n one jam. Don't forget I'm dependin' on 'em t'night."

The black horse rolled his eyes and snorted. Then he jingled the bit impatiently and quickened his stride. Rance scanned the shadowy loom of the mountains ahead.

A discouraged slice of a moon climbed painfully over the eastern crags, paling the golden stars to silver, flooding the rolling prairie with ghostly light. It was well after midnight.

Other stars pricked through the black shadows ahead. Golden stars that did not pale as the moonlight drenched them. Rance checked the stallion's pace somewhat as the golden stars grew larger.

"That'll be Paloa," he muttered. "Lots of lights for this time o' night. Looks like they're celebratin' somethin'. Mebbe we can help 'em to make her a bit livelier."

He pulled the horse to a walk before he reached the outskirts of the town. Hoofs making little or no sound, the black ambled between rows of dark houses. Now and then the *adobe* wall of a garden straightened out and lowered the ragged line of the roofs. Ahead lights glowed.

Rance began to hear music—the strumming of guitars, the rippling notes of song. Then the tap and shuffle of dancing feet, the clink of glasses and the slithering whisper of cards.

The blank windows gave way to gleaming squares. The voices of men and women tumbled merrily through the doorways. Figures passed and repassed the slanting bars of light.

Rance tied his horse at a convenient rack, loosened his guns in their holsters and crossed the street to where a wide-flung door beckoned. He had little fear of attracting undue attention—roving cowboys, miners, prospectors and such were too common to cause comment. The only danger lay in recognition.

He entered the *cantina*, narrowing his eyes against the sudden glare of light.

The saloon was well crowded. Men lined the long bar from end to end. Card games were going on at several tables. A roulette wheel whirred steadily. Couples whirled on the dance floor.

Rance bought a drink and leaned against the bar, sweeping the room with a searching glance. He tossed off the drink and left the place: nothing of interest here.

The same applied to the next place, and the next. At two others, smaller and less crowded, he merely glanced through the door.

"Hell," he growled, "looks like I dealt myself a hand from a cold deck!"

A Mexican in a ragged *serape* sidled up alongside him. He purred a sentence in soft Spanish.

"The *senor* is a stranger here, *si*?" Rance replied cautiously.

" 'Sposin' I am?"

"I thought," said the Mexican politely, "he might be seeking diversion, entertainment."

"And if I am?"

"Then," explained the other, "the *senor* assuredly should go to Miguel's *cantina*; Carmencita dances there tonight."

"Who's Carmencita?"

The Mexican shrugged his shoulders until the ragged blanket nearly slipped from around them. His hands spread wide in an expressive gesture.

"Ah, indeed is the *senor* a stranger! He knows not Carmencita? *Valgame Dios*! He knows not the sun of morning! He knows not the moonlight caressing the cheek of the rose with silver kisses! He knows not the dying stars singing together in the pale light of dawn. He—"

"Hold on!" snorted Rance. "You been eatin' *loco* weed? What you talkin' 'bout, anyhow?"

"*Senor*, I talk of Carmencita. Will not you come and see?"

"Hell, guess I'll hafta," Rance told him. "Trail yore rope, feller, I'll be right on yore trail. Wait a minute till I get my hoss."

Straight through the town the *peon* led. To where the lights were fewer and the music less. He turned into a side street, rounded another corner and paused.

"This, *senor*," he said, "is Miguel's."

The *cantina* was a big one. It sprawled along the street in an ungainly haphazard fashion. Light glowed softly through the recessed windows. Equally soft music seeped through the smoke-golden haze of the light. Rance could hear subdued laughter and the patter-murmur of voices.

"All right, let's go in," he told his guide.

The *peon* hung back. "But no, *senor*, 'Miguel's' is not for such as I. 'Miguel's' is for great *senors*, and their *senoritas*. I but show the way to those who know not 'Miguel's'. If the *senor* could spare—"

Rance chuckled and handed the fellow a *peso*.

"*Gracias, senor! Muchas gracias!*" A white-toothed grin splitting the dark face, a flirt of the ragged *serape*, and the *peon* was gone.

"Off to drop his loop on another *gringo*," Rance grinned. "Wonder what we'll find in this *hacienda*?"

The door was ajar. Rance pushed it open and entered. He sauntered to the bar, which stretched all the way across one end of the room, and ordered a drink. The bartender nodded pleasantly but offered no comment. Evidently gringos were not so uncommon in "Miguel's" as to cause question.

As he sipped the golden *mescal*, Rance searched the room from under the low-drawn brim of his wide hat. He could see that it was pretty well occupied, but the lights were dim and he could make but little of the faces of those seated at the various tables. His attention centered on a flashily dressed Mexican lounging to one side of the cleared dancing floor.

"That jigger looks like a rainbow what's got tangled in a flower garden," Rance told himself.

The Mexican *was* gorgeous. His pantaloons, tight-fitting, low-cut vest and flowing cloak were of green velvet. Down the front of the cloak and the front of the pantaloons were broad yellow stripes on which were embroidered roses, pansies and tulips, life-sized and of brilliant color. Snowy white shirt, black tie, flat black velvet cap and fancily stitched boots completed his costume. A guitar hung from his neck by a yellow ribbon.

Slender brown fingers brushed the strings. The guitar sobbed out a quivering melody. Then a voice like the sparkle of ruby wine:

"Open thy casement, dearest, unto the dove,

"For 'tis my soul that's seeking for thee, my love!"

"Whe-e-ew!" breathed the Ranger, "a feller what can sing like that's got a right to wear any kinda clothes he takes a notion to. He—"

The unspoken word flipped out of his mind and died forgotten. Rance drew a deep breath.

Onto the dance floor a girl had floated. She came from out the shadows like a shaft of starlight from behind a cloud. Her tiny feet seemed barely to touch the boards. Silken ankles gleamed amid the froth of her tossing skirts. Her arms and shoulders glowed white-gold under the soft lights. She was small and slender, with great dark eyes and tossing short dark curls.

Eyes narrowed, jaw grimly set, Rance Hatfield stared at her.

"Gypsy Carvel!" he muttered. "Ain't she *never* gonna give that sidewinder up! No wonder she didn't show at the trial! But what's she doin' down heah posin' as the dancer Carmencita?"

12

As the girl danced, Rance noticed that most of her glances went to a table a little apart from the others and nearer the bar. The Ranger divided his attention between the girl and that table.

Three men sat at the table. Two wore the flashing uniform of officers of the government army. Rance wondered what they were doing here in the stronghold of the rebel, Fuentes.

The third man was swarthily handsome, with a tremendous spread of shoulders and gorilla arms. Rance eyed him speculatively.

"Somethin' darn familiar 'bout that *hombre*," he mused. "I've seen him somewheah."

The big man turned his head, revealing a livid scar that gashed one ear from top to lobe and slanted down his neck. Rance swore softly.

"Tomaso Fuentes hisself! This is gettin' interestin'."

The friendly drink juggler leaned across the bar.

"*Ai!* she is *una bellisima moza!*"

Rance nodded. He heartily agreed that "Carmencita" was "a very beautiful girl." The bartender sighed.

"*Ai!* but she has eyes for none but *un Gran General!*"

This time Rance did not nod. Instead, he frowned. The idea of Gypsy Carvel having eyes for no one but "the big General," meaning Fuentes, did not meet with his approval. He called to mind some of the vicious practices and abominable cruelties credited to the revolutionary.

"Pig!" he growled as Fuentes gulped his glass.

"Eh?" exclaimed the startled bartender. "I see no *puerco*, *senor*!"

"Yore eyes ain't pinted right," chuckled Rance. "How come the little lady's got such a leanin' toward Fuentes?"

The bartender glanced furtively about, saw that the attention of all was fixed on the dance, and leaned closer.

"There is a whispered story, *senor*, a story that says Carmencita whose name is not Carmencita at all, came to Fuentes and begged of him help. She offered him gold, the story goes, but Fuentes shook his head. 'Dance for me in "Miguel's",' said '*un Gran General*'—Miguel is but Fuentes' manager, *senor*—'and perhaps we shall come to terms'."

"Then what?" asked the Ranger. The bartender leaned still nearer.

"Night after night she danced, *senor*, and night after night Fuentes sat and watched. The time grew short, and Carmencita grew desperate, for Fuentes would not name his price, nor would he promise to help. Then, the morning of yesterday, when Carmencita had all but despaired, Fuentes named his price."

"Oh-huh, and that was—"

The bartender glanced toward the dark-eyed girl floating and swaying in time to the music, graceful as the wind of dawn amid the flowers. His eyes slowly left her and focused on the Ranger's lean, bronzed face.

"*Senor*," he whispered softly, "the price was—*herself!*"

Rance Hatfield turned upon the Mexican a glance bleak as wind sweeping across snow-sifted ice.

"Feller, why you tellin' me this?"

The dark eyes met his squarely. "*Senor*," said the Mexican, "a worm looking up from the mire might love a rose, and never hope to possess it. Still, the lowly worm would not wish to see the rose crushed and befouled by the foot of—a *pig!*"

Rance nodded grimly. "I see; but wheah do I come into this?"

"They who ride the range for Arizona are brave men, and resourceful men," murmured the bartender with apparent irrelevance.

Rance's eyes narrowed still more.

"So the jigger knows I'm a Ranger," ran through his mind. "Well, he must be on the level, or he'd hardly tip his hand this way.

"What'd *La Senorita* have to say 'bout it?" he asked aloud.

The bartender shrugged. "What could she say? Fuentes is crafty. He gained her confidence—he can be most charming and courteous when it is necessary to be such to gain his ends. This room—the town—is filled with his men. *La senorita* learned she was a prisoner, helpless. She fought for time—insisted that first Fuentes must do the thing she asked. He consented, for it amused and pleased him to do it. To do it was to injure those he hates. Yesterday, as the day changed to night, he did it. Tonight he plays with her as the cat plays with the mouse. Tonight he demands his price."

Rance thought swiftly. "Feller, can you get outa heah without anybody askin' questions?"

"Assuredly, *senor*, I often go out on errands."

"All right. My hoss is tied acrost the street—the big black one at the little rack by hisself. Get that hoss untied and lead him over to this side the street. When I pitch *la senorita* out the door, you grab her, get on that hoss with her and hightail for the Border."

"And you, *senor*?"

"Nev' mind me. I'll be right on yore tail, if things go right. I'll take one of them other hosses. 'Fraid to take a chance with the girl on one of them. Mine's gentle and'll carry double 'thout makin' a fuss. If I don't catch up with you 'fore you get to the Line, you head straight for Ranger headquarters. Tell Captain Morton what happened. He'll look out for you and *la senorita* till I get theah."

"*Si, senor*, I go now. *Adios*."

"So long."

The bartender called an assistant, who lounged by the back bar, spoke a word to him and shuffled out the door.

Rance hammered the bar. "Fill 'em up," he mumbled blearily. "Have one on me."

The assistant grinned, and complied. Rance tossed off the *mescal* like so much water. "Hell," he shouted, "thass got no kick—make the next one *tequila*! Have 'nother one on me! Who-o-o-oppe-e-e!"

Occupants of the tables turned, frowning at the racket by the bar. The singer missed a note. Rance tossed off his glass of fiery *tequila* and roared for another. He staggered about to face the tables.

"Ev-body drinks on me!" he whooped, jingling a gold piece onto the bar. "Set up the house!"

The frowns changed to grins. Free drinks was something else. "If the drunken *gringo* was willing to pay for his fun, why let him have it!"

Waiters hurried forward with empty glasses, and hurried back to the tables with them filled.

"Drink up! Drink up!" howled the Ranger. "We gotta have 'nother round!"

Another gold piece clinked on the bar. The drink dispenser opened fresh bottles.

The music had stopped. The dancer stood listlessly waiting for the hurrying waiters to clear the floor. Rance spun a coin to the musician.

"Play somethin' quick an' dev'lish!" he ordered.

The grinning Mexican swept into the lilting roll of a fandango. Rance reeled across the floor.

"C'mon, lady, less dance!" he whooped, sweeping the girl into his arms. From the tail of his eye he saw Tomaso Fuentes frown angrily and half rise from his seat. But the crowd howled with glee and the revolutionary evidently thought better of his first impulse to interfere.

The girl was stumbling and reeling in the Ranger's staggering embrace. Rance read recognition, astonishment and pain in her dark eyes.

"For heaven's sake, let me be, you drunken beast!" she panted.

Rance lurched and whirled toward the door, yelping a wordless accompaniment to the music.

"Listen," he snapped between yelps—"gettin' you outa this—hoss outside—ride like hell—to the Border—un'stan'?"

He heard her breath catch sharply. Then she whispered, "Yes! Oh, thank God!"

Faster and faster drummed the music. Wilder and wilder grew the Ranger's whoops and leaps. The crowd was still laughing, but Fuentes' face was darkening with an ugly scowl.

Rance whirled the girl clear off the dance floor and right opposite the door.

"Steady!" he hissed, "you're goin'!"

"But you! What—"

"Be right behind you. All right—*out!*"

A bound and he had reached the door. He kicked it open, saw the bartender's form looming in the shaft of light. He hurled the girl into his arms.

"*Adelante! Muy presto!*" he shouted.

The bartender "went very quickly." Rance saw the two figures vanish from the light, heard the black horse snort. He whirled to face the roaring *cantina*, both guns coming out.

Men were boiling toward him, Tomaso Fuentes in the lead, snarling with a rage that was frightful.

"Hold it!" shouted the Ranger as *El Rey*'s hoofs thundered away from the building. "I don't wanta hurt you fellers if I don't hafta!"

A knife droned past his ear. Somewhere in the back of the room a gun boomed. Rance heard the whine of the passing slug. Fuentes was throwing down with a big gun.

The Ranger went into action. He kicked a table over, crouched behind the heavy oaken top and let loose with both guns. A man with a knife poised for the throw went down. One of the gaily clad army officers dropped his drawn gun and grabbed at a broken arm. Tomaso Fuentes went behind a table like a rabbit into its burrow. His bullets drummed against Rance's protection.

The crowd gave back, huddling against the far wall, the fight out of them. Only Fuentes and the remaining officer kept up a steady fire.

Rance smashed the army man's shoulder with a bullet from his left-hand gun. He took careful aim at what he could see of Fuentes' head and pulled trigger.

"Gotcha!" he exulted as *"un Gran General"* reeled back. Rance half rose from his crouch, gliding toward the open door.

Crash!

The roof of the *cantina* split asunder, letting in great whirls and blazes of pain-streaked light. After them came rolling black clouds. Rance knew he was falling, but he never knew when he hit the floor.

The bartender's assistant, who had crept in back of the Ranger, snarled down at the prostrate form and poised his heavy bung starter for another blow. It was not needed.

The wounded army officer aimed a gun with his left hand, but Tomaso Fuentes, blood streaming from an ugly gash just above the line of his black hair, struck the weapon up.

"No!" he barked, "that ees too easy. Me, *I* will take care of thees stealer of women!"

13

Rance found coming back to consciousness an unpleasant business. A splitting headache, a devilish sickness in the pit of his stomach and a general "gone-to-hell" feeling.

He tried to sit up, and didn't have much luck. Then he realized that his feet were roped and his hands tied behind his back. He rooted his nose into a dirty blanket, hunched his legs and finally managed to back himself up against a board wall.

"Now wheah the hell've I got to?" he wondered, staring about the unfamiliar room.

"Sho' ain't that *cantina* wheah the roof fell on my haid," he decided, eyeing a rickety table, a broken chair and a rusty sheet-iron stove.

A hollow groan jerked his eyes about and centered them on a blanket-tumbled bunk built against an end wall. Something writhed under the blankets, heaved itself up.

"Bull bellerin' blue blazes!" grunted the Ranger.

A mat of frowzy hair, a cactus-patch stubble of whiskers and two wild black eyes met his gaze.

"*Quien es*? Who is it?" he demanded.

There came another groan, then a dismal eruption of Spanish profanity.

"That's right, podner, get it off yore chest. I feel jest the same way 'bout it."

"*Senor*, you too are tied?"

"If I ain't, somebody done hypnotized me inter thinkin' I am. What's the big idea, anyhow?"

"*Ai! Maldito! Caramba! Cien mil diablos!* Tomaso Fuentes!"

Rance nodded as best he could. "Uh-huh, mebbe he ain't a hundred-thousand devils, but he sho' is *one*, all right. What'd he tie you up for?"

The Mexican groaned again. "It was I, *senor*, who led those who rescued the bandit Cavorca from the clutches of the *gringos*. I was to bring Cavorca—may he be accursed and rest uneasy in his grave!—to Fuentes, who had use for him. Cavorca and *la senorita* who rode with us from Paloa, they—how you say eet—give us the slip. Fuentes was angry, *ai*, most angry. He strike me! He tie me up! He say he feed me to the rats. *Huy! Caspita! Fuego!*"

While the Mexican continued to groan and swear, Rance slid into a somewhat less uncomfortable position and digested the information he had just received.

"So that is what Fuentes did for 'Carmencita'," he growled disgustedly. "She bribed Fuentes inter sindin' a gang acrost the Border to turn Cavorca loose. She—sizzlin' sidewinders they said theah was a girl with that gang when they busted inter the co'ht house. I bet a *peso* she was that girl!

It was her rode away with him, sho' as hell. Then Cavorca sneaks off and she ambles back to Paloa. Bet she had a scheme figgered out all the time to leave Fuentes holdin' the sack. Anyhow, me, little Johnny on the spot, comes along and plays right inter her hand. Feller, of all the prize suckers, yore it! You risk slidin' inter Paloa tryin' to get a line on Cavorca. Then you fergit all 'bout what you come for and help his girl to keep from payin' a honest debt. And all you got to show for yore brightness is a lump on yore empty haid!"

The Mexican heard his best efforts at profanity totally eclipsed. He paused to listen.

"*Si, senor*, I feel just the same way about it," he said.

Rance stopped swearing and grinned.

"Anyhow, she sho' don't *look* like that kind of a girl!" he told himself.

An uncomfortable silence followed. The Mexican tensed in an attitude of listening.

"Somebody comes!" he hissed.

The door was kicked open. A giant of a man with a bandaged head entered. After him came several others. Rance grinned into the face of the revolutionary leader, Fuentes.

"Hi, Tomaso? You got a headache, too?"

Fuentes glared down at the Ranger. Then an evil smile writhed his lips back from his yellow teeth.

"Ha! you live! Eet ees most fortunate, although,

Senor Ranger, you will no doubt soon not think so. I am rejoice to see you not dead—yet. Soon you weel be dead, *si*, but not *too* soon. Ha! ha! ha!"

Rance felt a cold chill creep up his spine as the evil laughter rang through the room. The Mexican on the other bunk gave a howl. Fuentes strode to him and slapped him across the mouth.

"Save your yelps, you," he snarled in Spanish. "Soon you will have the greater need of them. When the time comes, see if you can scream louder and longer than will the *gringo*."

He barked an order to the men who had accompanied him. They shuffled forward, lifted Rance and the Mexican from the bunks and carried them through the door.

The setting sun was drenching the mountain tops with red gold and turkis-green gold and purest golden-gold, and by its light Rance saw that he and his companion had been imprisoned in a small, roughly constructed cabin.

"No wonder I'm thirsty and darn neah starved," he mused. "Been out most of the night and all day. Wonder wheah we're headed for? An ant hill, or a stake with a fire built 'round it?"

He believed Fuentes capable of either atrocity.

The cabin, Rance could see by craning his neck, sat on the lower slope of a mountain. All about were rocks and spiny cactus plants and desolation. He was being carried up the slope.

A dark opening loomed in the face of a beetling cliff. The bearers paused. Matches scratched. The bearers resumed their march.

By the dim flare of candles, Rance could see rock and earthen walls shored by rotten timbers. The timbers arched overhead.

"An old mine tunnel," he deduced. "Now what the hell—"

On and on stumbled the bearers, panting with their loads. Rance could hear Fuentes cursing them and urging speed. They entered a cutting that criss-crossed the main tunnel, turned into another, and still another. Finally before a door of heavy timbers they paused. Rance heard the rattle of keys, the creak of rusty hinges. The bearers shuffled forward a few steps. Fuentes called a halt. Rance and the Mexican were flung carelessly onto the rock floor. Fuentes bent over the Ranger, the candlelight glinting on his evil eyes.

"*Adios*, *Senor* Ranger," he purred. "When comes the sharp little teeth to keep you company in the dark, think you on how you make the fool of Tomaso Fuentes. Think—and pay!"

The candles withdrew. The door crashed shut. The Mexican prisoner gave one terror stricken yell as the darkness closed down like a sodden blanket, and began to whimper.

"Figgerin' on leavin' us to starve," Rance grunted, straining at his bonds. "Well, we'll see 'bout that. Shut up, you!" he shouted to the Mexican. "We ain't dead yet and we won't be for a long time."

"Teeth!" screamed the Mexican. "Little teeth, sharp in the dark!"

"What the hell you talkin' 'bout?" demanded the Ranger.

The Mexican jabbered incoherent Spanish that Rance could not follow. The Ranger could hear him thrashing about.

"Scared so bad he's done gone plumb loco, I guess," Rance decided. "Now if I can jest work a hand loose."

He strained and tugged, but whoever had fastened the knots new his job.

"That jigger could hawgtie a lightnin' flash with a live rattlesnake," the Ranger panted. "Gosh, I'm numb all over from bein' roped up so long. Wrists is all bleedin', too. Wonder if I could talk that yelpin' lunatic inter tryin' to chaw me loose. Nope, that's out—it's a hair rope and his teeth couldn't cut it in a month. Gotta think of somethin' better'n that."

For long minutes he lay thinking, with no results.

The Mexican was babbling wildly. Suddenly his voice rose in a shriek of pain and terror.

"They come!" he screamed. "*Oh, Cristo!* they come!"

Rance swore roundly. "Shut up!" he roared. "What's comin'?"

"*Mira*! Look!" howled the Mexican.

Rance looked, and felt his hair prickle. In the darkness, ringing him about, were dozens of fiery points of light. Points that slowly moved closer. He could hear a faint slithering on the stone.

"What is it?" he shouted. The Mexican thrashed and kicked.

"Rats, *senor*, giant rats! They starve here in the deserted mine. They are bold from hunger! We shall be eaten while yet we live. *Dios*! Already they nip me!"

His thrashings redoubled. His screams rang from the rock walls.

Rance jerked convulsively. A sharp, stinging pain had shot along one of his bound wrists. The famished rodents were closing in. Cold sweat broke out on his forehead. He gulped back a mad urge to yell and scream even as the Mexican was doing.

"God!" he gasped, "I gotta do somethin'!"

Another sharp sting in his wrist. He rolled wildly onto his back, crushed a squeaking writhing thing under his weight and lunged away from the wriggling horror. Blazing sparks of light glared right into his eyes and he jerked his head back as teeth clashed together a fraction of an inch from his cheek. He felt that in another instant he would go stark mad.

"Gotta keep movin'," he gasped, rolling over on his face.

As he did so, something gouged sharply into his breast. He winced from the pain, wondering what it could be. Remembrance rushed to his aid and with it came a wild hope. Over and over he rolled, until he barged into his thrashing companion. The Mexican gave a louder yell of terror.

"Listen!" Rance thundered in his ear. "Shut up and listen to me!"

The other's howls died to gasps and pants. "I listen, *senor*, I listen!"

"Get yore haid over heah 'gainst my shirt front!" Rance ordered. "Rip the pocket off with yore teeth. Theah's a box of matches in it. Get holt of that with yore teeth, if you can. Hustle!"

Grunting and groaning, the other did as he was told. Rance felt the pocket tear loose. A moment of nuzzling and prodding. Then—

"Uh-wuh-unk!" mumbled the Mexican.

"Steady," cautioned Rance. "Hang onto it till I get holt of it with *my* teeth. Soon as I do, sink yore fangs into this handkerchief round my neck and pull it over my haid. Drop it on the ground. Damn them brutes! they're chawin' my legs!"

Rance got the match box in his teeth. He snuggled his head down and in another moment the handkerchief came jerking and snaking over it. He rooted his face down until he could feel the soft stuff where it lay on the rock floor. Then he began chewing madly at the wooden match box.

Splinters raked his gums. In his mouth was the taste of sulphur. A rat bit his cheek. Another tore at one of his hands. Then he got a match head squarely between his front teeth.

He crunched down on it with a quick grinding motion. There was a burst of flame, then a blinding flare in his eyes and a lancing pain in his mouth as the whole box caught fire.

Onto the big handkerchief Rance dropped the blazing box. The rats squealed away in terror. The Mexican screamed. The cotton caught fire.

With desperate haste, Rance hunched and wriggled until his bound wrists were against the flaming cloth. The smell of burning hair rope and scorching flesh filled the tunnel. Rance set his teeth, cold sweat popping out on his forehead, his body shivering with pain.

Grimly enduring the agony, he held his wrists against the fire. The blaze flickered, died down, winked out. Rance gave a mighty heave that sent torture coursing through his veins.

The charred rope stretched, crackled, ripped apart. Panting and gulping, the Ranger relaxed.

"*Senor*," quavered the Mexican, "they come back!"

"To hell with 'em," growled Rance, fumbling at the cords that held his ankles, "we got 'em licked. I'll have you loose in a minute."

Once on their feet, a few well directed kicks disposed of the rats. The rodents fled squealing into the holes from which they had been drawn by the smell of flesh and blood.

"Now," said Rance, "let's get the hell outa heah. Damn! I feel like I'd been put through a sausage grinder piece at a time!"

The Mexican was examining the door. He found a few overlooked matches in his pockets and struck one. He shrugged despairingly as the flare showed the massive timbers and the heads of big studs that clamped a heavy bar in place.

"*Senor*," he said, "I fear we are doomed. The door is fastened on the outside. We can never break it down."

"We won't try," Rance told him. "We'll find some other way outa this rat nest."

One of the Mexican's matches started them off down a low-roofed winding tunnel.

"Save the rest of 'em," Rance counselled. "We may need 'em bad 'fore we get out. Hope we'll find some water soon; gosh, I'm hungry!"

"The rats they eat us, soon, *por Dios*! we be glad to eat the rats!" groaned the Mexican.

As they floundered on and on through the black dark, Rance began to fear his companion might have the right idea. Water was the pressing need, however. The Ranger's throat was like an oven. His tongue was swelling. His scorched lips and wrists added to his sufferings. The Mexican was in little better shape, having been held prisoner even longer than Rance. He began to mutter incoherently and pushed ahead of the Ranger.

"Take it easy, feller," Rance cautioned anxiously. "You might fall in a hole or somethin'."

The other laughed wildly and staggered on.

"This damn tunnel leads right straight to Hell, I guess," swore the Ranger. "Well, it'll save us the trouble of doin' any back-trackin' when we cash in. What's yore name, pardner?"

"Angel," the other replied.

Rance chuckled mirthlessly. "They won't even hafta change it—jest hand you a harp and let you keep trailin' right along."

The Mexican began to laugh—wildly, hysterically. The low tunnel rang dully to his maniacal mirth. Rance shivered in spite of himself.

"Shut up, you *loco hombre*!" he shouted. "You'll have me pickin' things outa the air, too!"

"Ho! ho! ho!" roared the madman. "Is it not droll, *senor*? We—"

There was a prodigious splash, a strangled yell and then Angel's voice, perfectly sane and badly frightened.

"Help, *senor*, help! I am carried away!"

Instinctively Rance darted forward. Without the least warning, the ground vanished beneath his feet and he found himself struggling in deep swift water. He went under, gulped, strangled, and broke surface again.

"For Pete's sake!" he sputtered, "I wanted a

drink, but it waren't nec'sary to pour a river down my neck. Wheah are you, Angel?"

A gurgling squall somewhere in the darkness ahead answered him. Rance struck out strongly, guided by a spouting and thrashing. His out-reaching hand touched something and in another instant he had Angel by the collar.

"Stop yore damn kickin', 'fore I bust you one!" he panted. "Keep still and do as I tell you."

The Mexican quieted and Rance kept their two heads above water without much difficulty. He did not attempt to breast the current, which ran like a mill race. A tentative try to right and left brought him up against smooth rock walls.

"Runs through a cross tunnel," he reasoned. "If this gali-wumpus hadn't been makin' such a racket we'd have heard it and not tumbled inter it."

Angel's teeth were clicking together like dice in a darky's hand.

"*Senor*," he gasped, "I freeze!"

"I ain't so hot myself," Rance admitted. In fact the icy chill of the water was worrying him more than a little. There was more than discomfort in the cold—there was a deadly threat.

"I'm gettin' numb already," ran the Ranger's thoughts. "All I can do right now to hang onto this ground-flyin' cherubim. A little more of this and—good gosh! what's that?"

They had spun around a bend, scraping the rock

wall an instant and then shooting back into the middle of the stream. Completely blocking the tunnel ahead was a sheet of intense white fire, growing brighter as they swept toward it.

"*Madre de Dios*!" howled Angel. "Already we are dead! The flames of *El Infierno* await us!"

For an instant Rance was inclined to agree with the Mexican; then he understood and his whoop of joy rang between the narrow walls.

"It's the sun!" he shouted. "It's jest comin' up and shinin' right inter this damn roofed river. Feller, we're out!"

Angel's answer was a terrified yelp as they went plunging over the lip of a fall. Down they shot, beaten, hammered, half-drowned. They struck the deep pool beneath the fall and were pounded almost to the bottom by the rushing water. When they broke surface again Angel hadn't a yell left in him. He did have quite a bit of water, however.

The stream below the fall was swift but shallow. Rance waded to shore, dragging the gurgling Angel by the collar. Once on solid ground again, he took the Mexican by the middle and shook most of the water out of him.

"That oughta hold you," he decided at last. "Now wheah the hell are we, I wonder?"

Angel got up, still gulping.

"*Senor*," he quavered, "I know. I recognize that range of low hills to the left. Beyond those hills is a trail which will lead us to the home of a friend of mine. He will give us food and provide you with a horse. You can reach the Border then in but a few hours."

"What you gonna do?" Rance asked as they scrambled up the hill. "Can't go back to Fuentes, can you?"

"God forbid! Never do I wish to see his face again. Nor the faces of my companions, nor of any *bandido*. *Senor*, beside you walks a changed man. *Por Dios*! When I have rested I start for Sinaloa, far to the south. There my old father and my brothers till the soil and live in peace. I too will till the soil and find peace. Cursed be the day I left it to seek adventure!"

"That's right, feller," Rance chuckled, "you try and live up to yore name from now on."

Angel's friend proved to be a *chacerero*—the owner of a *chacra* or small ranch. He received the famished pair with true Mexican hospitality, fed them, treated their numerous cuts and burns and bites and bruises and dried their clothes. Three hours later, feeling like a new man, though deadly weary and gaunt from lack of sleep, Rance rode a borrowed horse to the Border.

14

Rance found Captain Morton at Ranger headquarters, a worried man. His most pressing concern was relieved when Rance turned up, but he still had plenty to get off his chest.

"Cavorca makin' a successful break that way after bein' convicted of robbery and murder has kicked up one devil of a row," he told Rance, after the Ranger had recounted his experiences. "Jim Thomas and Walsh Patton are workin' like pack rats in a sack of buttons. They got a petition goin' to present to the legislature when it meets. And I heah they got plenty of signers. Petition says the Rangers is nothin' but a burden on the taxpayers, ain't needed and don't do no good. They're playin' up Cavorca's get-a-way big. He's their ace-in-the-hole."

Rance nodded gravely. "Uh-huh, and he's our ace-in-the-hole, too."

"What the devil you mean by that?" demanded Morton.

"Jest this, Boss. Thomas and Patton and their crowd is tien' their whole case 'gainst the Rangers on Cavorca gettin' away. With Cavorca hawgtied, the whole thing'd tumble down like a *adobe* stable in a flood. All we got to do is get Cavorca again."

Morton snorted like a bull in a pepper patch. "Uh-huh, thass all!"

Rance Hatfield leaned forward, his gray-green eyes cold as mountain water flecked with snow.

"Boss, I'll get that horned toad if I hafta ride a gunpowder hoss through Hell to do it. Jest turn me loose on him is all I ask."

"All right," Morton sighed. "You got him oncet. Mebbe you can do it again. If you can, you'll save the Rangers. Governor Murphy is our friend, and he b'lieves in the Rangers. If we can show him that hyderphobia skunk Cavorca, nicely corralled 'hind a set of iron zig-zags or with daylight shinin' through him, Murphy'll be able to whip the legislature into line and give Patton and Thomas the run-a-round. If we can't! Well, feller, guess you and me can go back to punchin' cows for a livin'! Theah's times when I wish I'd never quit! Now you fergit all 'bout it and pound yore ear a while."

A trifle diffidently, Rance asked a question:

"That girl, 'Carmencita', wheah'd—"

"Hell, all this worryin' knocked it clean outa my mind—'most forgot to tell you," Morton interrupted. "Yore Mexican barkeep showed up all right—I'll have him heah when you come 'round t'morrer—but the girl! Well the way the barkeep tells it, right after they crossed the Line she dropped her handkerchief or somethin' and asked him to get it for her. Soon as he's on the ground, she slips inter the saddle and away she goes. Nope, not back inter Mexico—nawth on the Canyon Trail. Barkeep had a tough time leggin' it heah. 'Fraid he's lost most o' his faith in female human nature."

"Uh-huh, and it looks like I lost the best saddle bronk I ever owned!"

Rance slept the clock around and awoke stiff and sore but otherwise feeling fine. He got on the outside of a stack of flapjacks and a flock of cackle-berries and hustled to headquarters.

"Now ain't *that* fine!" he exclaimed as he sighted the building. "Anyhow she ain't no hoss thief!"

Seated on the board sidewalk was the Mexican bartender, holding the reins of *El Rey*!

The Mexican's teeth flashed white in his dark face. "*Ai Capitan*, it is good to see you! The *caballo*? *Capitan*, last night a *vaquero* rode to the door of the *casa* where I sleep, knocked and rode off most quickly. Going to the door I behold the black *caballo*."

Rance was staring at *El Rey*'s saddle and bridle.

"Good gosh! what a hull!" he exclaimed. "Hand tooled and mounted—and look at that silver mounted bit. Sa-a-ay—"

The Mexican grinned and bobbed. "*Si, La Senorita* forgets not, nor is she ungrateful! Only the *caballos* of great *caballeros* are so equipped, *Capitan*. But *El Capitan* is himself a great gentleman. Should not his *caballo* bear only the best?"

Still slightly dazed, Rance hunted up Captain Morton.

"Sit down," said the captain, "got any plans?"

"Uh-huh," Rance nodded. "I think I've figured somethin'," he added before Morton could interrupt. "I callate Cavorca give Fuentes the slip so's he could get his own men t'gether fust and meet Tomaso on more've an equal footin'. But they'll get t'gether, all right, and 'tween 'em they'll cook up a fine kittle of hell. Cavorca'll be needin' money bad and he'll hit some place this side the Border."

"The question is wheah?" worried Morton.

"Don't think theah's so much question 'bout it," said Rance. "He'll go wheah he figgers he can make the biggest killin' and get away with it."

"And that's—"

"Silver City, suh."

Captain Morton pounded on his desk. "Damn'd if I don't believe yo're right!"

The tall young Ranger stood up, flexing his long arms. "Guess a little ride is what I need to limber me up," he said, "so if it's O.K. with you, suh, I'm headin' for Silver City."

Like a hell-kettle set out to cool—and not cooling—Silver City crouched on the shoulder of a grim mountain. High over the huddle of tents and shacks and false-fronted brick buildings loomed the great peak, dwarfing them, making them appear grotesque and sordid and ugly, casting its mighty shadow across the blistering desert that stretched away to the eastern skyline. Dust storms boiled up from the desert, flung against the mountain wall and sifted back onto the roaring town. The blazing Arizona sun turned it to showers of gold. The cold, dead desert moon caused it to gleam with the frosty gleam of the silver bricks that men trundled down the loading platforms of Silver City's giant stamp mills.

Dust from the desert and silver from the mountain! That was Rance Hatfield's thought as he and the Mexican bartender, Pedro Hernandez, rode into Silver City late one afternoon.

Rance had seen Coffin and Concha and the other Arizona hell-roarers, but Silver City could give them cards and spades and best them hands down. Silver City was the wildest, maddest, most turbulent town the Ranger had ever entered. Life was cheap in the mines, and men who were used to brushing fingertips with death by day cared little for his frozen grin at night.

Blood and whiskey and gunsmoke and gold! Mix 'em up, and add a dash of lust and cruelty and greed! It made a grand devil's-brew. Silver City rank deep!

From end to end of the town ran the great Alhambra silver lode. Dozens of mines gutted the mountain of its treasure. Under Silver City was another city—a city of timbered galleries extending hundreds of feet into the ground. From that underground city came the veined ore that was Silver City's life-blood. Men slaved and mucked and sweated and died in that underground city. They rioted and fought and drank and played and died, in the city seething above the gloomy galleries.

Then, too, the great C. & P. railroad was stretching steel fingers across the desert. Rawhidin' Dave Barrington and Jaggers Dunn were building a double-track line to the rich cattle and farming land beyond the scorching sands and the mountains. Silver City was now headquarters for the construction forces.

Cowboys riding north with their trail herds also stopped at Silver City, coming and going.

The cold-faced gamblers, the oily saloon keepers and the hawk-eyed women of the dancehalls welcomed miner, railroader and puncher alike. A sprinkling of Mexicans and Apache halfbreeds added spice to the mixture. Silver City whooped 'er up and threw the keys away!

"She's Dodge, Tombstone, Poker Flat and Deadwood rolled inter one and set a-fire," Rance said as he and Pedro stabled their horses. "Now, feller, yore job is to circ'late 'round through the Mexican section and see what you can find out. Most of Cavorca's men is Mexicans and the odds are better'n even he'll have Mexican scouts gettin' the lay of things heah. Shavin' off yore whiskers and moustache oughta stop anybody from knowin' you, but keep yore eyes open, and remember, you and me is jest a coupla waddies on a cel-bration. Don't you get too darn drunk and go to talkin', though; and watch out for the *senoritas*."

"Assuredly, *Capitan*, will I watch out for them," grinned Pedro as he sauntered through the stable door, *sombrero* tilted rakishly over one eye, ever-present cigarette drooping from his lower lip.

"Now jest what did he mean by that?" chuckled Rance. "Well, I got a notion it'll take a smooth little *muchacha* to get the best of Pete."

By the time Rance had washed up and stowed away some chuck, the lovely blue dusk of the desert land had snared mountain and sands in a net of beauty whose fringes reached trustingly toward the garish town, only to be beaten back by the hard blaze of lights flaring from saloon and dance-hall and gambling hell and brothel. Overhead, the bonfire stars of Arizona shuddered away from the bedlam of song and yell and curse and groan that spouted up through the darkness.

Spilled whiskey stained the sawdust and spilled blood reddened the whiskey. Men fought over drink or gold or women—or fought just for the fun of fighting. Women laughed with painted lips, and calculated shrewdly with eyes that laughed not at all. White-faced gamblers spoke briefly from the corners of their mouths, and raked in the gold that miner and railroader and cowboy had salted with the sweat of heartrending toil and now tossed away with a curse and a jest and a careless shrug. Silver City boomed defiance to the laws of man and the laws of nature—and got away with it!

"Is she allus as wild as this?" Rance asked a friendly puncher who stood, glass in hand, at the bar beside him.

"Feller," drawled the waddie, "you ain't seen nothin'! T'morrer is payday for the mines and the railroad. They're jest tunin' up the fiddles t'night. T'morrer night the orchestra cuts loose!"

Rance drifted from saloon to saloon, listening, watching. He heard and saw plenty, and some of the sounds and sights very nearly put a curl in his black hair; but as the roaring hours of early evening slipped away to make place for the "roaringer" hours of midnight and after, he had learned nothing relative to his quest.

"Hope Pete's havin' better luck," he growled as he trudged up the hillside.

15

Rance found Pedro Hernandez in his tiny room near the livery stable.

"You find out anythin'?" he asked the exbartender.

Pedro nodded. "*Si*, not much, but something. There are strange men, lately arrived, in the Mexican quarter I am told by one who lives there. Among them, said she, are *Norte Americanos*, in appearance most evil."

Rance pondered this information gravely, his black brows drawing together over his cold gray eyes.

"It ties up," he mused. "You know, Pete, after Cavorca robbed the Curry bullion train and murdered the guards, I trailed him for months 'fore I finally dropped my loop on him. I slipped inter Mexico oncet, to his hangout down theah, and tried to snake him out and get him acrost the Line. I saw Americans in his outfit then—plumb salty *hombres* they was, too. Yeah, what you found out ties up all right."

For some time, he sat silent, while Pedro smoked. Abruptly he straightened up, his thin-lipped, good-humored mouth tightening. In his ears rang the words of the friendly cowpoke in the saloon. *"T'morrer is payday for the mines and the railroads!"*

"Pete!" he exclaimed, "how you figger they bring in the money they use to pay the miners and railroaders with?"

Pedro reflected. "The Tucson stage I would say, *Capitan*," he hazarded at length.

Rance nodded. "Figger you got the right of it. Nobody's s'posed to know, but of co'hse ev'body does, 'specially them what ain't got no bus'ness knowin'. The stage lays up overnight at Burley and makes the trip through Bleached Bones Canyon by daylight. Gets in heah right after noon. Uh-huh, that's it, Peter. Well, I'm gonna pound my ear a hour or two—got a ride ahead of me this mawnin'."

16

It is not a nice place, Bleached Bones Canyon. Not only because of its frowning black walls and its foaming white water that ever gnaws hungrily at the narrow strip trail wandering about between fangs of rock. Too many terrible things have happened in the stone-cramped gorge that, even at noonday, is always shadowy. There are too many shattered skeletons shimmering whitely, too many rusty stains that look like dried blood, though they are really only iron outcroppings. Enough blood has been shed in there to make the white water run red. Men ride through Bleached Bones Canyon with furtive glances and their chins slanted over their shoulders.

Old Frank Masters, driver of the Tuscon stage, was nervous. His glance shifted continually from the trail ahead to the ragged crest of the beetling wall "t'other side the crik" and back again. From time to time he gazed back along the way they had just travelled. He growled querulously to the heavily armed guards who sat on either side of him.

"I tell you theah's a feller been follerin' us ever since we hit this damn hole-in-the-wall. I don't like it!"

"Never saw anythin' you did like," grunted lanky Jim Osborne.

Fat, jolly Tim Mooney chuckled. "Responsibility sets heavy on Frankie's shoulders," he piped. "He's allus seein' bandits when he's haulin' payday gold."

" 'Sponsibility, hell!" yelped Masters. "I'm 'sponsible for nothin'. I'm hired to drive stage, and that's all. What happens to that damn gold is up to you tailbone warmers. Jest the same I don't hanker to get a slug through my gizzard."

"Drivers never get shot," chuckled Tim.

"Hell, no," grunted Osborne. "None of 'em wuth shootin'. Heah's the south end of the canyon, you ol' grumble-growler, and nothin' happened."

"Jest the same I got a feelin'," snorted old Frank, "I got a feelin'."

Riding along less than a quarter-of-a-mile behind the stage, Rance Hatfield also "had a feelin'." He was puzzled, too.

"I'd a swore they was gonna pull somethin' t'day," he told the black stallion, "and this canyon's the place to pull it. Guess that hunch was a maverick. All open trail to town and the bank, now. Well, feller, we had a nice ride, anyhow."

He glanced at the sun slanting down the western sky and quickened the stallion's pace. "If them jiggers in front don't hustle, payday is gonna be late t'night."

The Silver City bank squatted near the north end of the town's principal street. It was a bulky one-storied building with thick walls, barred windows and heavy doors. A sign on one of the windows read "Closed for the day," but the front door opened as the stage pulled up.

Rance saw the two messengers lug a heavy, iron-bound box into the bank. Peering through a window as he rode slowly past, he saw them heave it onto the shelf of a grated opening. A clerk back of the grating was writing a receipt.

Rance was just about to ride on when the clerk moved slightly, into a shaft of afternoon sunshine pouring through a side window. Rance saw the light glint on hair more golden than the sunshine itself. The "clerk" looked up and the Ranger stared into a face as handsome and as evil as must have been that of Lucifer, "Star of the Morning," when Heaven's gates crashed shut behind him.

Rance hit the ground running and went through the bank door like a greased pig through a bowlegged men's convention. Manuel Cavorca, crouching in the teller's cage, saw him coming and greeted him with a roaring gun. Rance's answering shot knocked the iron-bound box sideways. One of the guards clutched it and it crashed to the floor, outside the cage.

Instantly the building seemed to explode with the thunder of six-shooters. The two guards went down, dead hands clutching their half-drawn guns. Rance hurled himself sideways back of a pillar, his Colts beating a drum-roll of fire. Men boiled out of the open vault, from behind desks, from underneath tables. The Ranger's fire blasted them back from the cages. Outside sounded the shouts and yells of the aroused town.

Manuel Cavorca, calm, collected, barked an order. The back door banged open. There was a clatter of running feet, a thumping in a nearby stable; then the quick thud of galloping hoofs.

Rance dashed out the front door in time to see *El Rey* careening up a side street, blood streaming from a bullet furrow on one glossy black haunch. The bandits were already a cloud of dust on the southwest trail. A crowd of townspeople were clamoring down the street.

"Get in theah and see to the bank folks," Rance shouted, and set out after his horse.

The stage guards and two bandits were dead. The bank workers were found trussed up in the vault.

"They jumped us right at closin' time," explained the cashier. "We didn't have a chance."

On the floor outside the cages was the payroll money box, its contents intact.

"Wheah's that tall black-haired jigger?" squalled old Frank Masters. "If it hadn't been for him they'da got away with it. He blew 'em clean out from 'tween their ears. What a *hombre*! I nev' *seed* sich nerve or sich shootin'!"

"Who was it?" asked the cashier.

The stage driver described Rance as he remembered him, and from that description Captain Morton himself would not have recognized his star Ranger.

For which Rance was duly thankful. His least desire was to become conspicuous in Silver City—just yet. To do so would be to make his work all the more difficult. He was bitterly disappointed at the outcome of the bank raid. True, he had blocked the robbery and saved the big payroll; but Cavorca had escaped. To advertise the part he, Rance, had played in the affair would be to give Thomas and Patton more ammunition to use in their fight against the Rangers.

"They'd beller like steers with the colic 'bout Cavorca slippin' outa the loop," Rance assured himself. "They'd make folks forget all 'bout the payroll and it'd end up by the Rangers bein' blamed for them two pore devils of guards gettin' drilled. Nope, the only thing what'll do any good is Cavorca hisself as Exhibit A, either stuffed or on the hoof."

Pedro Hernandez, however, suffered from no illusions.

"*Ai, Capitan*," he enthused, "it must have been a fight! Such a fight as *El Capitan* fought in the *cantina* at Paloa. Why did you not take me with you, *Capitan*?"

"Yore a darn sight more good to me circ'latin'

'round and findin' out things," Rance told him. "Learn anythin' more?"

"Only this," said Pedro. "The night before the attempt at robbery there was a *senorita*, a most lovely *senorita*, asking questions in the Mexican quarter. Finally one of the strange men met her and talked with her. Talked with great earnestness, shaking his head often. *La Senorita* wept, I am told, but the man continued to shake his head and she went away, where to no one knows."

"You know who she was?" Rance asked casually.

"No, *Capitan*," replied Pedro. "I did not see her. I only heard."

After Pedro had left, Rance sighed deep relief. "Well, anyhow she wasn't in on that stickup," he breathed thankfully. "Looks like she even didn't know it was bein' pulled off. Looks like she figgered Cavorca was up to some dev'lment, though. If it ain't hell—a girl like her wasted on such a wuthless sidewinder!"

The thought left him depressed and gloomy. "I'm goin' out and get me a drink, two drinks," he decided. "Little whirl with one of the dance-hall *ninas* mightn't go bad, either."

Ten minutes after leaving his room Rance decided that the friendly puncher in the saloon the night of the Ranger's arrival had known what he was talking about, even though he had missed the time by twenty-four hours. The "orchestra" was going full blast tonight.

Payday had been postponed because of the robbery attempt and the disappointed workers were making up for lost time.

"All the mines is closed down," a bartender told Rance. "Theah ain't enough men left in the railroad camps to bile a pot o' beans, and a flock of punchers who took three big trail herds nawth last month jest got inter town. Looks like it's gonna be the biggest night Silver City ever seed."

It was. That night Silver City reached such heights of madness and plumbed such depths of evil as she never achieved before or since. The very Gila Monsters and rattlesnakes of the desert at her feet would have died of poison had they sucked in the venom of that night.

Silver City's streets ran red with blood and lust and passion and greed. Gold glowed in steady streams across the bars. The tables of the gamblers groaned under its weight. The women of the dance-halls clutched it greedily in the early hours of the night, and flung it away in wild abandon before the red dawn flamed upon the mountain tops. Men died with spilled whiskey staining their shirt fronts and the paint from hot lips staining their souls. The gold was crusted with sweat and black with dried blood. Tobacco smoke and gun smoke swirled in the air. The gleam of silver flashed answer to the gleam of steel. The death cry of a poor devil with a knife in his back and a clutching hand in his pocket was drowned by song roared from a throat that would be bubbling with blood before the first sun shaft kissed the desert.

"Whew!" whistled Rance Hatfield as he fought his way into a saloon. "If all I owned was this heah town and Hell, I'd sell her and live in Hell!"

From saloon to saloon he went, and ever the mad pace grew madder and the wild night wilder. The bartenders no longer pulled corks—they smashed the necks of the bottles and gushed the raw whiskey over the splinters into glasses with hands already pawing around them. The roulette wheels spun faster and faster. Men shoved their winnings back onto the red or the black without counting them, roared exultantly if they won again, shrugged and grinned if they lost. Dice clicked, cards whispered one against the other. The stiff white collars of the dealers were no longer white nor stiff. Their faces, formerly white and cold as the collars, were flushed and mottled and streaming sweat. Only the silk and tinsel of the dance-halls seemed to gleam the brighter as the hands screeched around the clock.

"Funny how much better lookin' a dance-hall girl gets after you've looked at her a few times through the bottom of a whiskey glass!" Rance chuckled as he swung a slim, flaming-haired partner across the sanded floor.

Suddenly the Ranger stiffened. A face had drifted past, a swarthily handsome face topping a tremendous spread of shoulders.

"What's the matter, cowboy?" asked the girl.

Rance ignored her. Some hidden monitor in a corner of his brain was clamoring for attention.

"Now wheah've I seen that jigger before?" he muttered. "Why'd he give me such a start?"

He followed the big man with an intent gaze. The other glanced straight into the Ranger's face. Recognition flamed in his eyes, he whirled about and Rance saw a jagged livid scar slanting down his neck. *Tomaso Fuentes*!

A mad thrill shot through the Ranger's brain. Tomaso Fuentes! Not even Cavorca himself was more wanted by the Arizona authorities. Fuentes was red to the elbows in American blood. His frequent raids across the Border were things of terror and horror. Once let the Territory of Arizona lay hands on him and his conviction and execution were swift and sure. Capturing Fuentes would be a Ranger triumph as great or even greater than the capture of Cavorca.

Rance hurled the girl from him and bored across the room, shoving cursing dancers aside, driving straight for *"un Gran General,"* who was driving just as straight for the outer door.

Rance jerked his gun but dared not shoot. There were too many men and women in the way. That did not bother Fuentes, however. He slewed sideways, flame gushed from his low-held hand.

A girl screamed, a wild shriek of agony. A man went down, coughing and spitting. Rance gritted his teeth.

"The hyderphobia skunk! Just let me line sights on him—jest once!"

Fuentes shot again, and Rance felt the wind of the bullet that knocked the back-bar mirror into a thousand splinters. Fuentes knocked a girl down, clubbed a man with his gun barrel and tore the swinging doors off their hinges going through. Rance hit the board sidewalk a split second later.

Up the street was a swirl and eddy where "*un Gran General*" ripped the crowd apart, his big shoulders and his flailing gun barrel clearing a path for him. The angry revelers, closing in his wake, hampered the pursuing Ranger. Men struck at Rance, others sought to seize him, not knowing what it was all about. He tore free from their clutching hands, fended their blows as best he could and grimly stuck to Fuentes' trail.

"*Un Gran General*" had gained a long lead, but now the crowd was thinning. Rance risked snapping a shot or two over their heads with the only result that his quarry ran the faster.

Up the long slope of the mountain toward the mines, where the lights were fewer, the street practically deserted. Ahead loomed the gaunt buildings of the great Alhambra mine. To the left were those of the Golconda. To the right straggled ramshackle structures of smaller diggings.

Rance knocked Fuentes' hat off with a whining slug. The fugitive ducked frantically, swerved to the right and darted into a shaft housing. Rance heard the watchman's challenge, then a groaning yell, a clash of levers and the whine of moving machinery. He barged the door open and leaped into the dimly lighted building.

Directly in front of him yawned the mine shaft. High over his head the huge barrel of an old-fashioned windlass, its speed controlled by crude but efficient grippers, turned slowly. In the gloom of the shaft a wire rope swayed and jerked.

"Sidewinder started the cage, jumped in and's goin' down the shaft!" Rance panted.

He leaped to the lever that controlled the descending cage. Before he reached it the rope ceased swaying. The cage was at the bottom of the mine.

"Damn!" swore the Ranger. " 'Fore I can get that contraption up and down again he'll have time to dig a hole through to China. Heah goes nothin'!"

Measuring the distance across the yawning shaft he gathered himself together and leaped. He caught the rope with one hand, slipped, dangled, got another grip just as his fingers tore loose. He wrapped his legs around the swaying cable and went down hand over hand through the black darkness.

He hit the cage top with a crash, lost his grip and rolled off to the ground, the breath almost knocked out of him.

A gun blazed a yard-long lance of fire and a bullet screeched through the space a standing man would have occupied. Rance jerked his gun, sent two bullets smashing at the flash and rolled frantically aside. An answering slug knocked rock splinters into his face.

Deafened by the roar of his own guns, he dimly heard the thud of running feet. He leaped erect, tripped over a projecting timber end and went sprawling. By the time he regained his feet once more the quick thudding had died away in the distance. The gloomy passages of the mine were silent save for the soft drop of water and the groan of timbers settling under the terrific compressing force of the mountain resting upon them.

For an hour or more Rance prowled through the underground galleries fruitlessly. Fuentes had found either a snug hiding place or another exit. Rance was inclined to think the latter. Finally he made his way back to the shaft.

The cage had been drawn up, but a few yells brought it down again. The watchman, with a sore head and a sawed-off shotgun, greeted Rance when he reached the surface. He peered closely at the Ranger, the ten-gauge ready for business.

"Wheah'd you come from, and wheah'd that damn greaser go?" he demanded.

Rance told him as much as he thought necessary. The watchman commented vigorously and profanely.

"Chances are the horned toad found the tunnel openin'," he concluded. "Yeah, theah's one; hits the air over clost to the Alhambra workin's. Mebbe he'd been heah b'fore and knowed wheah to look. We work a lot of Mexicans. What's good for this gun-barrel headache?"

The first kiss of dawn was blushing the mountain tops as Rance made his way back down the slope. A merciful darkness still shrouded Silver City crouching like a drunken hag over a broken gin bottle. Sodden figures lay in the streets. The sobbing moan of a dying man quavered up from somewhere among the shadows. There were huddled forms under the gambling tables, beside the drenched bars, stark in blotchy doorways. Bits of tawdry tinsel and torn silk littered the dance-hall floors. The hanging lamps smoked and guttered, ghastly in the welling torrent of golden light from the east. A vile stench tainted the air.

But clean and sweet and lovely with an unearthly loveliness, the desert stretched its shimmering arms to the dawn. The great mountain blazed rose and red and scarlet and gold as its purple sleeping robe slipped down its majestic form. Water leaped silver and white. A whisper of wind danced across the crags and the sand. A bird sang—and it was day!

17

Rance found Pedro in his room, pacing the floor with excitement. He burst into voluble Spanish.

"Hold on! Hold on!" cautioned the Ranger. "Take it easy, feller, I can't make head or tail what yore talkin' about."

Pedro gulped, ceased his prancing and returned to English.

"The sheriff and his posse. They pursued Cavorca."

"Yeah, I know," said Rance. "Fat chance they had of catchin' up with him."

Pedro gestured expressively. "Thees sheriff, he not so dumb. He attempts not to catch up with Cavorca. Instead he rides to the west, circles the Canyon Trail and rides north on it, figuring that Cavorca would turn into the Canyon Trail and ride south."

"Not so dumb, that," agreed Rance. "Did he meet him?"

"Yes and no," explained Pedro. "Cavorca he not dumb, either. He have scouts riding ahead. They see the sheriff and his posse. They warn Cavorca. The bandits ambush the posse and kill or wound several. Not enough, however. Now the south mouth of Dead Man's Canyon is closed to Cavorca. He dares not ride back north."

"How you learn all this, Pete?"

"The sheriff sent a man here for food and help. Everybody drunk. Not yet has help been sent to the sheriff."

"Uh-huh, and while they're foolin' around, Cavorca'll squirm out someway," growled the Ranger. "C'mon, Pete, you and me is ridin'."

Several miles north of Mexico the Canyon Trail enters the gloomy gorge from which it gets its name. The inner walls of Dead Man's Canyon are steep and rocky, clothed with dense chaparral and manzanita. From the ragged rims the ground falls away abruptly in almost straight-up-and-down slopes. The canyon, in fact, splits the crest of a mountain whose precipitous sides are its outer slopes.

Night was not far away when Rance and Pedro entered the gorge. *El Rey* had not fully recovered from his flesh wound and Rance forked a sturdy brown pony hired from the livery stable. The Mexican rode a bay.

"Heah that?" exclaimed the Ranger. "They're shootin' it out in theah, Pete."

Faint fire-cracked explosions tossed back and forth between the rock walls, punctuated by duller thuds.

"Six-shooters and rifles both goin'," deduced Rance. "The sheriff musta got tired of waitin' and decided to close in on 'em."

Pedro nodded and for some minutes the pair rode in silence. Rance turned to his companion, jaw tight, eyes gleaming under his black brows.

"Pete," he said, "you and me is gonna bust up the party and give the sheriff the break he's needin'."

"*Si, Capitan*, but how?"

"This way. Cavorca will be worried 'bout his back trail. He'll know if the sheriff gets help it'll come this way. Chances are he'll have scouts posted to warn him if another posse is comin'. He don't dare lead his gang back this way with the sheriff campin' on his tail. Once in the open country he's sunk and he knows it. I'm bankin' on the scouts gettin' rattled if they see or heah anybody comin' from the nawth. You and me is goin' in hell-bent-for-leather, shootin' and yellin'."

"*Si, Capitan*, a good plan."

"Uh-huh, if it works. If it don't—well, hope *El Rey* gets a good new boss!"

The popping of pistol shots grew louder. Rance loosed his guns, gathered the reins in his left hand. Ahead loomed a projecting buttress of rock where the canyon curved.

"All right, Pete, heah we go!"

Spurs drove home. The horses shot forward, stormed around the turn.

"Come on, fellers, heah they are!" whooped Rance.

Pedro gave a yell that would have put an Apache buck to shame. The guns of both let go in a crackling fusillade.

Answering shots from the canyon side kicked up puffs of dust at their feet. There was a startled yelping amid the chaparral, then a clatter of hoofs.

"It's workin'!" exulted Rance. "Shoot, Pete, shoot!"

On they swept, iron hoofs striking showers of sparks from the rocks. Rance stuffed shells into his empty gun while Pedro took potshots at the fleeing scouts.

"*Ha!*" shrilled the Mexican. "*Capitan*, look!"

The hillside was suddenly a-swarm with frantically fleeing men. They rose from behind boulders, darted from clumps of manzanita. Some tried to urge their horses up the steep slope, others held their hands high in the air and howled for mercy. Puffs of smoke zoomed up from the canyon ahead. A deep voice bellowed orders.

"Sheriff's tellin' his men not to shoot them what gives up," Rance shouted.

More hands went up. Rifles and revolvers clattered on the rocks. The bandits had had enough.

"*Maldito!*" shrieked Pedro. "Cavorca! Cavorca!"

Rance saw the outlaw leader break cover at the same instant. Straight up the slope he urged his magnificent golden sorrel. Beside him rode a slim little figure on a bright roan. Rance groaned as the posse in the canyon sent a volley after the fleeing pair.

The slender rider beside the golden-haired bandit suddenly threw up fluttering little hands and pitched headlong from the saddle.

"God!" breathed the Ranger.

Manuel Cavorca glanced down at the crumpled little form in the mesquite. For an instant his grip seemed to tighten on the reins. Then a feeble hand gestured frantically toward the saffron-flaming crest of the gorge. Cavorca bent low over the sorrel's neck and sent him leaping up the boulder strewn slope.

"The dirty sidewinder!" grated Rance. "Left her! High-tailin' it to save his own wuthless hide.

"Pete!" he barked, "don't let him cut back this way. Block the nawth end!"

Up the slope went the chunky brown pony, snorting and slipping.

"If I only was forkin' *El Rey*!" groaned the Ranger.

The brown horse was doing the best he could, but the sorrel gained steadily. A lucky smooth stretch gave the pony a momentary advantage, but the sorrel had almost reached the crest when he was still a hundred yards behind.

Cavorca twisted in the saddle. His blue eyes glinted along a pistol barrel. Rance saw the puff of smoke and heard the thud of the bullet reaching its mark at the same instant.

Down went the brown horse, dead with hardly a struggle. Rance kicked his feet loose and hurled himself free. He struck the ground hard, but was on his feet in a single rolling bound, just in time to see Cavorca vanish over the crest.

"Gonna ride down the outer slope—he'll never make it," gasped Rance, floundering and stumbling up the hill.

But Cavorca did. Rance reached the lip of the canyon as the sorrel went down a final hair-raising stretch, "sittin' on his tail." Cavorca turned, waved a derisive hand and vanished amid the thick growth.

Slowly, haltingly, the Ranger walked back into the canyon, his tortured eyes dreading what he knew they would all too soon see. The old sheriff panted up to meet him.

"Cavorca get away?"

Rance nodded dully. The sheriff wiped his damp forehead with a red handkerchief.

"His gal's down theah," he gestured, "by that clump of mesquite. Dyin'."

With a face of stone, Rance Hatfield walked to the mesquite clump. Under a blanket a slight figure writhed and moaned. The Ranger hesitated, then strode to the blanket.

"God-a'mighty!"

With incredulous gaze he stared into a dark

lovely face from which two great hate-filled eyes glared up into his. Lips that had been rose-red were now gray with pain. The dying girl hissed a sentence in Spanish.

Rance knelt. "*Senorita*, who are you?"

The dark, agonized eyes blazed. "Me, I am Teresa. *Perro*! did you keel my man?"

"Yore—yore man? You mean Cavorca?"

"*Si*, Manuel, my sweetheart. I am hees woman."

Slowly the Ranger shook his head. "Cavorca got away," he replied softly.

Joy replaced the hate and suffering in the black eyes. "*Madre de Dios*, *gracias*! Now I die happy."

Rance bent lower, voiced a question:

"Teresa, wheah is Gypsy Carvel?"

Hate flamed in the dark eyes once more. The girl levered herself up on stiff arms.

"Geepsy! She ees—"

Blood gurgled in the slender throat, choking the words. The tense arms relaxed.

Rance caught her and eased her gently back upon the blanket. For a long moment he stared into the half-open eyes. Then he softly drew a corner of the blanket over the quiet face.

18

"Well, we rounded up the gang, anyhow," said the sheriff as he and Rance rode back to Silver City together.

"Uh-huh," grunted the Ranger pessimistically, "and Cavorca got away. Like cuttin' the haid off a tapeworm and bottlin' the body. Haid goes right on growin' 'nother body."

"You figger Cavorca'll get 'nother outfit?"

"Shore he will, and he won't waste no time 'bout it, either. He'll be out to even up t'day's score in a hurry."

The sheriff looked worried. "Mebbe he's got his belly full of Silver City," he offered hopefully.

Rance was not impressed. "Mebbe, but the chances are he'll figger he jest got a onlucky break this time—which is 'bout the truth of things, come to think on it. Chances are he'll still callate Silver City's easy pickin's."

They rode in silence for some time. The Ranger broke it at last.

"What's botherin' me most right now, sheriff, is Tomaso Fuentes. That slash-necked sidewinder didn't ride all the way to Silver City, takin' chances on the Border Patrol pickin' him up, jest to hoss it in a dance-hall. He's stewin' up some kinda kittle o' hell or I'm a sheepherder. I sho' wish I knowed if he left town."

Rance found Silver City suffering from a headache, but busy. The thunder of the stamp mills shook the air. Buildings vibrated to the faint boom of blasts set off far beneath them in the timbered galleries of the mines. Ore wagons jammed the streets, their drivers lifting the hair from the mules' backs with profanity that caused the air to smell of sulphur. Carts loaded with portly silver bricks stuck in the ruts and were cursed and levered out.

"One thing the outlaws don't have no luck stealin'," a mine official told Rance. "We cast them bricks in two-hundred-pound weights. They don't go so well on the back of a hoss."

The days six-sevened into weeks and another payday approached, but nothing was heard or seen of either Manuel Cavorca or Tomaso Fuentes. Nor of Gypsy Carvel.

"Anyhow," he sighed in relief, "it wasn't her what shot Old Man Blanton back theah in the Cochise co'hthouse. Them bandits we caught all 'grees that was *Teresa*. If any of 'em knows anythin' 'bout Gypsy they won't spill it. I got a notion that big tough *hombre* what told us all t' go to hell is hep to somethin'. His eyes sorta squinted when I said her name, but theah's 'bout as much chance of gettin' anythin' outa him as theah is of gettin' a cowpoke inter Heaven."

One thing still worried the Ranger greatly. "Even if she wasn't in on the co'hthouse raid, it was jest about as bad if she hired Fuentes to do it."

Thinking along these lines, he asked Pedro a casual question.

"For what did *La Senorita*, Carmencita, make the bargain with '*un Gran General*,' *Capitan*?" replied Pedro. "Why, it was like this—"

"*La Senorita* owned a *chacra*, a small ranch, in our Mexican state of Sonora. She suddenly desired money, most urgently, it would seem. She gathered together all her cattle into a trail herd and started driving them to market. The government, on some pretext, seized that trail herd. *La Senorita* was in despair. Her need for money was great. She endeavored to hire Tomaso Fuentes to take that herd from *El Presidente*'s men and run it into Arizona. It pleased Fuentes to do so, for he hates *El Presidente Diaz*, and he greatly desired *La Senorita*. The rest of the story, *Capitan*, you already know."

Rance solemnly shook hands with Pedro, much to the Mexican's astonishment.

"All clear as a hatful of mud now," he told himself exultantly. "Easy to see what she wanted money for. Cavorca had jest so much time to appeal his conviction to the higher co'ht, and appeals cost money. Callate Fuentes didn't even know that she wanted the money. Snakin'

Cavorca outa the co'hthouse was Fuentes' own notion, I bet a *peso*. He needs Cavorca."

There came a night of wailing wind and lashing rain. Rivers cascaded down the mountainsides. The desert soaked in the moisture and glimmered ghostily with a light of its own making. Everybody who could remained indoors.

Pedro Hernandez was not one of these. He scuttled into Rance Hatfield's room after midnight, dripping water and excitement.

"*Capitan*," he chattered, "*La Senorita* rides this night to the meet with Manuel Cavorca! Hasten, *Capitan*, hasten!"

"Hold on," exclaimed Rance. "Wheah'd you learn all this?"

Pedro explained volubly. "My friend in the Mexican quarter she have a brother. The brother he drank with the man who bore the message from Cavorca. The man boasted that he was Cavorca's *hombre*, told of the message, after my friend had smiled upon him. She is a wise *nina*, my friend."

"Did she find out wheah they was gonna meet?"

"Assuredly, *Capitan*. They meet in Shadow Canon. Do we ride now, *Capitan*? *Viva*!"

19

Shadow Canyon is a box canyon. Several cattle trails run into it, for there is good grass and water in Shadow Canyon. Only one trail runs out of it, a trail that zig-zags dizzily upward along the western wall, barely wide enough for a single horse, winding around bulges and juts, with always the swirling black water of Shadow Creek gleaming hungrily beneath it. One looks into the mouth of Shadow Canyon from a tiny mesa half-a-mile distant. The mesa slopes rather sharply to the canyon floor.

The rain had ceased and the sun was casting golden spears into Shadow Canyon when Rance and Pedro reached the lips of the mesa. The Ranger peered intently toward the mouth of the gorge.

"Pete," he exclaimed suddenly, "theah's somebody ridin' down theah—two somebodies!"

"Three," corrected the Mexican, "a third comes from the south."

A grim drama was in the making at the foot of the mesa, but as yet neither Rance nor his companion realized it. They did not remain ignorant for long.

"That's Gypsy theah in the canyon mouth," Rance muttered. "She don't see that jigger ridin' 'round the grove toward her. Is it Cavorca? Don't look like him from heah. Theah he goes outa sight behind the trees!"

Pedro exclaimed sharply.

"*Capitan*, the man from the south rides a golden horse."

"That'll be Cavorca," growled the Ranger, "but the other one—sufferin' sidewinders! It's Fuentes!"

The second rider had swept into view again, scant yards from where the girl sat her pony. Rance saw her whirl her horse into the canyon.

She was too late. Fuentes reached her side before the pony got fully under way. He reached out a gorilla-like arm, swept her from the saddle and flung her across his own pommel. Into the canyon thundered his tall gray horse, swerved to the left and began climbing the narrow trail that wound over the north wall of the box.

Down the lip of the mesa Rance urged *El Rey*, fully recovered from his wounds, Pedro crashing along behind him, but losing ground at every stride. Cavorca was forgotten. All Rance's energies were centered on overhauling the straining gray horse that crawled fly-like up the slanting trail.

"We gotta get him, feller! We gotta get him!" prayed the Ranger.

Across the foot of the mesa flashed a golden

shape, into the canyon and up the trail. Cavorca, too, had seen and was racing to the rescue.

"I nev' thought that hellion could ride in shootin' distance of me and be safe," Rance groaned, "but theah he goes! He ain't safe from Fuentes, though!"

"Un Gran General" had turned in the saddle. From his hand darted a puff of smoke and a flicker of pale flame. Again and again he fired, knowing that his pursuers would not dare shoot in return for fear of hitting the girl he held helpless in front of him. Rance gritted his teeth as Cavorca swayed in the saddle, but the outlaw kept riding.

"Wasn't plugged after all! He—damnation!"

The golden horse stumbled, went down. Its scream of pain and terror struck the Ranger's ears, a thin ribbon of sound, as it crashed over the edge of the trail.

Hurled from the saddle like a stone from a sling, Manuel Cavorca rushed down and down to the racing river seventy feet below. He struck the water with a sullen plunge and vanished.

Rance Hatfield, thundering up the dizzy trail, jerked *El Rey* to a staggering, plunging halt. Gun ready, he leaned in the saddle, peering at the rushing white water. But Cavorca did not reappear.

"Musta hit a rock," muttered the Ranger. "Guess that settles Manuel. Anyhow, Pete'll take care of him if he comes up. Get goin' hoss, we got another sidewinder to hawgtie!"

Fuentes was pushing his horse cruelly, raking its bleeding flanks with his spurs, pounding it over the head with his gun barrel, but the giant *El Rey* gained at every bound.

"Yore doin' it, feller, yore doin' it!" praised Rance. "Now if we jest get a break!"

Around a bulge careened the black horse. Less than fifty yards distant, Fuentes was aiming his gun.

Rance saw the puff of smoke, heard the scream of the slug that knocked his hat from his head. Fuentes' lips writhed back in a snarling curse, the barrel of the big gun dropped down again, steadied.

"He won't miss twict!" panted Rance. "Faster, feller, faster!"

El Rey overhauled the gray as if he were standing still. Fuentes, his face a livid mask of evil, held his fire.

"Waitin' until he's sure!" muttered Rance, crouching low on *El Rey*'s neck.

Fuentes' eyes gleamed, narrowed. Rance could see the muscles of his gun arm tense.

There was a sudden flash of a slim little hand. It struck Fuentes' arm just as the gun blazed. The bullet kicked dust from the canyon crest.

"Good girl!" whooped the Ranger, rising in his stirrups.

The gray horse snorted in terror as *El Rey*'s snapping teeth reached for his flank. He shied against the cliff side and at that instant Rance Hatfield left the saddle in a streaking dive. His reaching arms wrapped about Fuentes' huge shoulders and held. The cinches gave way under the strain and both men and the girl crashed to the rocky trail. Over them stormed *El Rey*, still trying to get his teeth into the gray gelding.

Crouched against the cliff, her head ringing from the fall, Gypsy Carvel stared with horror filled eyes at the death's struggle raging on the lip of the dizzy gulf. She saw Fuentes, foam flecking his bestial lips, sink his teeth in the Ranger's arm. She saw the spurt of blood as an iron-hard fist hammered his jaw and tore the yellow fangs from their hold. She saw the gorilla arms wrap around Rance's waist, tightening until his ribs crackled with the strain.

Over and over, rolled the battlers, kneeing, kicking, striking. Grimly silent they were, save for the sobbing of the breath from bursting chests. Breast to breast, glaring eye to glaring eye, fighting to the death for that which men have fought since the beginning of time—a woman!

Under Fuentes' chin Rance cupped his locked hands, jerking his knees up at the same time. He put forth all his strength, broke the other's hold and rolled free. Cat-like, both men were on their feet, circling warily.

Fuentes leaped, his huge right fist whizzing in, irresistible as a cannon ball. Rance weaved aside, stooped and seized the Mexican about the thighs. Groaning with the strain, he hurled Fuentes over his head.

There was a wild scream of terror as Fuentes cleared the lip of the trail and shot down, his arms and legs whirling in the air. Up from the rocks fanging the black water drifted a crunching thud!

As he peered at the motionless, broken body a hundred feet below, a mighty exultation thrilled Rance Hatfield. His work was done—better than well done!

As he stepped back from the edge, he felt a touch on his arm. He turned to face Gypsy Carvel.

"You—you are hurt!" quavered the girl.

Rance grinned at her through puffing lips. "Nothin' to make a fuss over. You all right?"

"Yes, but you are bleeding."

"Jest scratches. Be forgot in a day or two. Guess it's all over, *senorita*."

The girl drew a quivering breath. "My—Manuel?"

"Looks like the river got him," Rance told her soberly. "I never saw him come up."

Tears welled in the dark eyes. Her red lips trembled. But there was a note of relief, almost of gladness in her voice when she spoke.

"He went clean!"

"Yes, ma'am, he died like a man."

For a long moment they looked into each other's eyes. Then the Ranger spoke, hesitantly.

"Miss Carvel—Gypsy—can't we—"

For an instant a light leaped in the girl's dark eyes; then it was drowned by a shadow, a shadow of memory. Her voice was an ache of pain—

"You forget. There—there—is—is blood between us!"

She began to cry softly.

"I—I must be going now," she said. "Thank you for all you have done. Perhaps some day—"

For the briefest moment she clung to him, his bronzed hand caressing her dark hair. It was not strange that Pedro Hernandez, urging his foaming horse around the bulge, should misunderstand and grin hugely.

"*Ai*," murmured Pedro to himself, "but when the hand of a friend plucks the rose—*that* is different!"

Rance barked a question at him. Pedro shrugged expressive shoulders:

"Cavorca? He sweem down the river, strong. Me, I shoot once—and miss. Then a bend in the river. I ride fast to the assistance of *El Capitan*. I do right, *si*?"

"Yeah, you did right, I guess," sighed Rance.

"Hangin' onto that sorrel-topped jigger is like holdin' a greased eel in a barrel of lard! Well, it won't be long 'fore we heah from him again. You can jest bet yore last *peso* on that!"

20

Dawn was breaking across The Enchanted Mesa country. Pale blues and velvety grays were rolling back the hard blacks and purples that had marched under the bonfire stars of Arizona since the scarlet sunset. The mountain crests were ringed about with saffron flame that thrust shining spears into the royal robe of shadows still striving to cling to their mighty shoulders. *La Mesa Encantada* trembled under a crown of beauty. The flanks of a great dark peak trembled to a deep, vibrating hum that swelled steadily until it became a pounding roar.

The roar focused along the shimmering twin ribbons that were the tracks of the C. & P. railroad. It raced ahead of the huge locomotive that labored mightily up the winding right-of-way, her stubby stack thundering, her tall drivers spinning blurrily in the ever strengthening light.

Old Tom Mulholland, the 678's engineer, reached up and tugged at the whistle cord. The wailing notes tossed crazily to and fro among the cliffs. Old Tom leaned out the window and glanced back along the glinting yellow coaches of his long passenger train. The *Palo Pinto* Limited rocked and lurched as she crashed her mile-a-minute way toward Black Hell pass. High above the train, the overhung cliffs glowered threateningly.

Old Tom's gaze came back to those cliffs, to the crooked track ahead.

"Hell of a country for a railroad!" he grumbled to his fireman. "Some day it'll—*good God!*"

Like dust from a squeezed puff-ball, the cliff a scant two hundred yards ahead flew in all directions. As he frantically shoved the throttle shut and slammed on the air, Old Tom dimly heard the roar of exploding dynamite.

"Leave her, kid!" he yelled to the fireman.

With a sickening crash, the 678 hit the mass of splintered stone heaped across the track. Over went the giant engine onto her side. Down the steep embankment she slid and plowed and rolled. Old Tom died with one hand on the throttle and the other on his automatic brake handle.

The fireman, bruised and bleeding and groggy, saw the mail, baggage and express cars leave the track and bound wildly over the ties. They did not turn over. The mighty heap of shattered stone brought their crazy progress to a thudding halt. The fireman also saw yelling, shooting figures come leaping from behind boulders and ridges.

Up the embankment they stormed, straight for the careened express car. Their leader hurled something at the locked door—something that left a wispy trail of smoke behind it and exploded deafeningly. The door flew to pieces.

"Holy Pete!" gasped the fireman, "it's a robbery; they're after the money in the express car!"

Terrified passengers were boiling from the crumpled Pullmans. Shoving them aside came a stocky bronzed man in overalls, high-heeled boots and a wide hat. A long black gun glinted in his right hand. He sprinted toward the train wreckers, the gun spouting smoke and flame.

A bandit went down. Another shrieked and clutched a smashed shoulder. A third kicked and clawed his way to the bottom of the embankment and lay there in a silent heap.

The leader of the wreckers ran forward a few paces in front of his men. The first rays of sunlight glinted on his golden hair. His amazingly handsome face was twisted with awful rage. His blue eyes glittered back of the sights of the stubby rifle he held.

The rifle blazed. The stocky man in the wide hat crumpled up like a suit of old clothes, blood oozing from a ragged furrow just above his left temple.

"That's Wes Farley, an Arizona Ranger, they just killed!" whispered one of the huddled passengers.

The golden-haired bandit leader barked an order to his dark-faced followers.

"Take him!" gesturing to the wounded Ranger.

Two bandits, glowering evilly at the passengers,

glided forward, lifted the unconscious man and carried him beyond the engine and around a curve. Two others covered the passengers with their guns.

There was a shot inside the express car, and a scream. A little later the sharp bark of an explosion. Then another.

"The safes they are open," called a voice in Spanish.

The bandits worked swiftly, carrying sacks and bundles around the curve.

"They won't bother us," a passenger comforted his nervous fellows. "They're after big game—lots of money in that express car."

Last of all the golden-haired leader vanished around the curve. The passengers caught a final flash of his blue eyes as he turned.

"It's Cavorca, the Mexican outlaw and revolutionary, sho' as hell!" said the passenger.

"Don't look like no greaser," commented another.

"Ain't," said the first speaker succinctly. "American born—old Spanish family. Rangers thought they had him a coupla times, but he allus slips loose. Got a big follerin' below the line. Theah they go!"

Hoofs were thudding beyond the curve, dying swiftly to silence.

"Heah comes somebody else," exclaimed the fireman, pointing to a crest across the low-walled canyon through which the right-of-way wound.

A single horseman was riding along the crest. Riding with reckless abandon. As he came opposite the wrecked train, a gasp of startled amazement went up from the passengers.

"Good gosh! he's gonna try and ride down the cliff!"

It wasn't really a cliff, but steep enough and rugged enough to pass for one. The stranger, sitting his magnificent black horse with careless ease, sent the animal plunging and teetering down the hair-raising slope.

In a cloud of dust and rolling stone he reached the bottom and charged across the gorge. Panting and snorting the black horse toiled up the embankment.

"It's Rance Hatfield, the big he-wolf of the Rangers," exclaimed the passenger who seemed to know everything. "They say he's slated to be captain when Morton resigns."

The sweating horse topped the embankment. The Ranger swung to the ground and high-heeled toward the group.

"Tell me what all happened?" he asked.

They told him, volubly. He strode to the looted express car and stared at the quiet forms of the express messenger and his assistant. He gave the two dead bandits a casual glance.

"You sho' it was Cavorca's outfit?" he questioned.

"Nobody else," insisted the talkative passenger. "I seed him when he was on trial over in Cochise—day 'fore he busted jail. Nobody'd ever forget that face of his."

The Ranger nodded. "That's right. You say they took Farley with them?"

"Uh-huh."

"But he waren't daid," supplied another passenger hopefully.

Rance Hatfield's green eyes narrowed, his mouth tightened.

"Woulda been a hell's mercy if he was," he said softly.

Abruptly he strode to his horse, mounted and rode toward the curve beyond the dynamited cliff, the big black picking his way daintily among the shattered stones. The bruised and battered fireman watched him go.

"After seein' the way that feller looked, somehow I feel sorta sorry for Cavorca," he mumbled through his cut lips.

21

Rance quickly picked up the bandits' trail, and just as quickly lost it. Less than half a mile beyond the curve, the canyon sprawled into a jumble of buttes, low mesas and lesser canyons. The soil was iron hard, almost impervious to hoofs shod or unshod. Rance patiently quartered the ground, investigating canyons and gorges, but it was more than an hour before he hit upon the right track.

It was only a few drops of blood spattered on a white stone, but plenty for the trained eyes of the plainsman. From time to time other drops of blood appeared, then hoof marks in a soft place. Rance was grimly alert as he rode into a narrow canyon whose damp floor was deeply scored by a recently passing body of horsemen.

"Damn little more'n an hour ahead of me," he growled. "All right, hoss, get goin'!"

The black stallion snorted, slugged his big head above the bit and fled through the canyon.

Rance's watchful eyes suddenly noted a number of black dots wheeling and circling in the air a mile or so ahead.

"Vultures," he muttered. "Mebbe that wounded jigger they took along's done cashed in. Mebbe—"

The unspoken thought tightened his lean jaw still more. He scanned the trail ahead, dreading the sight that might at any instant be revealed to him. He was totally unprepared for the horror of the thing he finally did see.

The perpendicular walled canyon opened abruptly onto a stretch of sand and cactus and mesquite.

The vultures were wheeling and circling. One swooped low above the mesquite as the Ranger rode from the canyon, then abruptly planed upward again.

"Whatever they're after mustn't be dead yet," muttered Rance. "I wonder what—"

The words trailed off soundlessly behind lips suddenly stiff. Rance jerked the black horse to a halt with a roughness foreign to him, swung to the ground and walked swiftly toward a little mound. His feet scuffed to a leaden standstill and for a terrible moment he stood and stared.

The low mound was an ant-hill, from which the huge ants were swarming in millions—swarming onto the thing of blasted horror pegged across the hill. A pitiful thing that had once been a man! As Rance stared with graying face, an ant scurried into one empty eye socket and out the other! *And the man still lived!*

"God!" breathed the Ranger, and reached for his gun.

Lean jaw set like iron, lips still and bloodless,

he drew the heavy Colt for a purpose the horror of which he had never dreamed. With a hand that shook convulsively, he lined the sights on the almost fleshless skull. His finger curled on the trigger.

But the bullet of mercy was not needed. The half-eaten form suddenly stiffened, reared against the thongs that held it and relaxed. A dry rattling sounded in its bloody throat. The eyeless head lolled sideways and was still.

With a quivering sigh of thanksgiving and relief, Rance holstered his gun. He looked down upon what was left of the man who had been his fellow Ranger, his friend. The tortured form of dead Wes Farley seemed to cry out for vengeance. Rance raised somber eyes to the hard blue sky; his lips moved:

"God, mebbe *you* let Manuel Cavorca get away with this, but *I* won't!"

22

Captain Morton listened gravely to Rance's report, nodding his head from time to time.

"Pedro, my Mexican, got a tip that Cavorca had crossed the Line," Rance told him. "I was cuttin' 'crost country when I heahd the explosion. I figgered Cavorca might have somethin' to do with it and headed toward the sound. Got theah too late. You know how much they got off the train?"

Morton's face grew even more grave. "Rance," he said, "it's plain hell. Theah's a lot more to it than jest a train robbery. Theah was a Silver City bullion shipment on that train, Rance. The Silver City people were keepin' it dead secret, or thought they were. Nobody but the messenger was s'posed to know what was bein' carried. Hell knows how Cavorca got wind of it, but he did. Rance, theah was more'n a million dollars in that shipment!"

Rance whistled his amazement. "A million dollars! And Cavorca got it all!"

"Ev'ry last *peso*," nodded Morton. "Rance, you know what that means?"

"It's liable to mean most anythin'," guessed the Ranger.

Morton leaned forward and tapped the table

top with an earnest finger. "I'll tell you what it means. It means that Cavorca has at last got money to finance his revolution plans. It means fire and blood and gunsmoke below the Line and up heah, too. It means plain hell on both sides the border. Things are ripe for it down theah and the fightin' and the robbin' and the murderin'll backwash inter Arizona—plenty! It'll mean soldiers heah and more trouble because of them. It may even mean war 'tween the United States and Mexico 'fore it's finished. And who in hell's gonna stop it?"

Rance Hatfield stood up, and the dapper little Captain with the icy gray eyes noted how he seemed to tower in the low-ceilinged room. He spoke two quiet words:

"The Rangers!"

Morton grunted. "It's damn liable to finish the Rangers, too," he growled. "Walsh Patton and his Cochise crowd is still after our scalp. You downin' Fuentes that-a-way and bustin' up Cavorca's old outfit sorta put a knot in their rope, but this train robbery bus'ness'll give 'em somethin' new to work on. You got any plan?"

"Rifles," said the Ranger tersely, "they're what Cavorca is gonna need. He's got the men and he's got the money, but he ain't got near enough long guns. Now wheah's he gonna get them?"

"From this side the border," replied Morton instantly.

"Uh-huh," agreed Rance, "and wheah's he gonna get 'em t'gether and run 'em across?"

Morton hazarded a guess, "Silver City?"

Rance shook his head decidedly. "Nope, it's too easy to get 'em t'gether in Silver City and too easy to slip 'em across the Line from theah."

"Hell," protested Morton, "ain't them jest the reasons why he *would* use Silver City?"

Rance's only reply was a grin. Morton looked blank a moment, then grinned back.

"Uh-huh, yore right," he acknowledged. "Cavorca'll figger *we're* gonna figger him shippin' through Silver City, and he won't."

Rance nodded. "Jest the same, Boss, don't take no chance on Silver City. Put a good strong patrol theah and don't make no bones 'bout it. We'll block that hole and then Cavorca will sho' hafta hunt him another one; and I got a hunch I can drop my loop on the one he'll use. He'll ship through Brazos."

"Hell, feller, theah ain't no trail south from Brazos! The Black Hell hills is plumb in the way. He'd hafta run his string northwest fer clost to fifty miles and then swing south."

"Uh-huh, and what's to stop him? Theah ain't a town or even a ranch in that whole god-forsaken stretch. All he has to do is get outa Brazos ahaid of ev'body and foller the Canyon Trail. Theah ain't no way to cut in in front of him and theah's a hundred places along the trail one man could hold off a posse. Theah's somethin' else to consider, too: the Gandara ranch ain't far from Brazos, and Cavorca has allus sorta kept in touch with—with—" Rance could not bring himself to say it, after all. Morton said it for him:

"Uh-huh, with that cousin of his'n, Gypsy Carvel. Theah's gonna be a warrant served on that gal yet."

"She ain't never done nothin' contrary to law," Rance defended, "and she sho' saved my bacon a couple times."

Rance abruptly changed the subject. "Boss," he said, "I'm ridin' to Brazos."

"I'd jest about as soon be ridin' to Hell!" growled Morton.

Rance held something of the same opinion, but he kept it to himself. He found nothing in Brazos to cause him to change that opinion.

Sprawling in the shadow of the Black Hell hills, Brazos had mushroomed from a straggling cattle town that owed its existence to the fact that the C. & P. railroad had shipping pens there, to a roaring city of thousands. Gold was the reason for its growth—gold that men clawed out of the Black Hell hills. A year before, a gaunt prospector had staggered into Brazos, thumped a poke of dust on a bar and called for drinks for the house. Twenty men had followed him back into the hills and in less than a week twenty men thumped twenty sacks on the bar and fought for the privilege of buying drinks for the house.

That was the beginning. The devil alone knew what the end would be, and he wasn't telling.

Where, less than a year before, there was the single bar in which the twenty "old-timers" had wrangled, now there were a score of bellowing saloons that had thrown the keys away the day they opened. Gold poured into Brazos from the frowning hills to the south. Whiskey and women and gamblers and gunmen poured in over the trails from the north and east. Bearded miners, bronzed cowboys from the great ranches across which the trails ran, pasty-faced card sharps and dance-hall girls with calculating eyes rubbed shoulders in the crowded streets. Whiskey flowed like water. Blood flowed free as the whiskey. Gun smoke swirled coldly blue in the hot sunshine or under the blazing Arizona stars. Brazos glittered like a knife reaching for an unprotected throat and screeched like a paw-fast panther.

Into this welter of passion and lust and curses and song rode Rance Hatfield with two black guns tapping his muscular thighs and a warrant in his pocket.

"Manuel Cavorca—MURDER," read the warrant and Rance knew that the only way it would be served was at the muzzles of those black guns.

Only once did he run across a man who recognized him. Late one afternoon, while ambling along Crippled Cow street, he bumped into a white-bearded old fellow dressed in a rusty black suit and carrying a small black case.

"Why the hell can't you look wheah yore goin'?" sputtered the oldster. "You punchers—well, I'll be damned! Rance Hatfield!"

"Hold it, Doc!" cautioned Rance. "I'm s-posed to be a maverick heah. Wheah's a place we can have a little pow-wow?"

"I got a office down the street," replied Doc McChesney.

McChesney was a former coroner of Cochise county and Rance had last seen him at the county seat.

"I didn't run agin last election," Doc explained as he poured a drink. "People was gettin' too damn healthy over to the county seat and things was so plumb peaceful theah waren't nobody gettin' shot. I come over heah wheah a doctor can make a livin'. Been thinkin' of openin' a undertakin' 'stablishment, though—that's the best bus'ness in this town. Now tell me what the hell you doin' heah. Guess you know I can keep my trap shet."

Rance left the office with Doc an hour later and walked into another surprise.

The surprise, mounted on a pinto pony and riding swiftly out of town to the south, was slim and graceful with great dark eyes and wavy hair that caught and held coppery glints of sunlight. Rance stood in the middle of the street and stared, and had Gypsy Carvel looked anywhere but straight ahead she must have seen and recognized him.

"That's Jim Carvel's gal on that paint hoss," said old Doc, giving the Ranger a quick, keen glance.

"She's been livin' with her uncle, Alfredo Gandara, up to a month or so ago. All of a sudden she moved back to the Lazy-E ranch—that was Carvel's brand, you know. She moved her stock offen Gandara's range and started the Lazy-E workin' again. Guess that gold mine claim of hers on the Gandara place had brought in money enough to let her get the Lazy-E goin'. It's a darn good spread, all right, and I don't guess the big cattlemen hardly wanta start a war on a gal by herself. Most ev'body felt purty bad 'bout how the Hoskins-Carvel row turned out, anyway. I was coroner and made out Jim Carvel's death certificate, 'member?"

Rance nodded absently. He remembered, all right, but he was thinking of other things. Was there more to Gypsy's move than appeared on the surface? Why should she leave her uncle's comfortable home right at this time? Rance had not seen her since that day, months before, when Manuel Cavorca had vanished in the waters of Shadow Creek, although he had talked with

Alfredo Gandara and a couple of the Gandara boys.

Rance worried about the matter all the rest of that day. The following morning he saddled up and rode to the Lazy-E ranch, south of Brazos. For a long time he sat his horse in a manzanita thicket and watched the little ranch-house. He saw a couple of punchers ride away, and a Mexican woman of some three hundred pounds gross tonnage hang up a washing. Of Gypsy he saw nothing. Then something caught and held his attention.

Two men were riding along the trail that wound in the shadow of the Black Hell hills. They turned toward the Lazy-E ranch-house and Rance saw that they were flashily dressed Mexicans. They dismounted, jingled up the steps and knocked. Gypsy Carvel opened the door and stepped onto the porch.

The Mexicans swung their *sombreros* low in salute and started talking. The girl listened until they had finished and seemed to protest. She shook her head doubtfully as they earnestly urged something. Finally she appeared to give reluctant consent. The Mexicans bowed low again and rode away. The girl watched them out of sight and re-entered the house listlessly, her curly head drooping.

For a long time Rance Hatfield sat staring at the closed door. It did not open again and finally he turned his horse and rode away, carefully keeping the thicket between him and the house.

"Now what's the answer to that?" he wondered. "Them Mexicans is up to somethin'—somethin' that they need that girl's help with. She didn't want to give it. Looks like she had a notion that what they was proposin' waren't jest what they claimed it was. Smooth lookin' *hombres*, too. Wouldn't be a bit s'prised if they was puttin' somethin' over on her. But what?"

That night Rance saw the two dark-faced riders talking earnestly to the proprietor of a particularly vicious saloon whose trade was almost wholly Mexican. The Ranger, sitting in the shadow and sipping a glass of *mescal*, caught a word or two.

"Tomorrow night—when the moon has set—not many this time."

23

Sitting on his horse in the mouth of a dark alley the following night, Rance watched shadows moving about the rear of the frowsy saloon in which he had overheard the whispered conversation. It was too dark for him to see what was going on. When, a little later, hoofs clicked softly, he tightened his grip on the reins and spoke to the black horse.

A faintly darker blotch in the night, the big stallion eased out onto the trail. Trained to step softly, he picked his way among the loose boulders with uncanny ease. Rance gave him his head, knowing that he would follow the sound and scent of the geldings.

"They're slantin' south, feller," he breathed. "Begins to look like we made a mistake. If it was Cavorca's gun runners, they'd be swingin' nawtheast by now. Ain't no hoss livin' what can climb that cliff wall to the south. You sho' yore on the right track?"

A bit of open prairie a little later proved the soundness of the cayuse's judgment. Drifting along like swift shadows were a half-score of riders. Rance could even make out bulky packages tied back of the saddle cruppers. His eyes brightened and his jaw set a little tighter.

"Long guns wrapped in burlap," he deduced; "but wheah in hell are they takin' 'em?"

More and more to the south turned the ghostly brigade. The gloomy wall of the Black Hell cliffs began to jut up against the star net that Arizona calls the sky. Straight-up-and-down were those cliffs, forming a barrier that not even a mountain goat could climb. There were gorges and passes beyond them, but none clefting that somber granite battlement.

"Hoss, it jest don't make sense!" wailed the bewildered Ranger.

Rance rode through a grove and abruptly a single light glowed in the star-drenched dark. For a moment he was at a loss to account for it; then the solution thundered across his mind.

"The Lazy-E ranch-house! Now what? Are they—sho' as yore a foot high they are, hoss! They're turnin' toward the ranch-house. Now this *does* beat hell!"

From the shadow of the same thicket that had sheltered him the day before, Rance saw the men ride to the ranch-house and dismount. They began fumbling at the bundles their horses bore.

A shot rang out. Another, and another. The dismounted men seemed all yelling together. Rance saw the ranch-house door swing open in a blotch of yellow light. Boots clattered on the porch as men leaped for the shelter of the building. Others tried to mount the plunging horses. Some succeeded and rode madly into the night.

From the shelter of a nearby grove swept a tight group of riders, shooting and yelling. They charged toward the ranch-house and were met by a storm of bullets. Red flashes spurted from windows and doorway. Then the door slammed shut as the foremost of the raiders flung themselves onto the porch. Rance heard a woman scream.

The Ranger went into action like a thunderbolt. Guns blazing, he charged the group milling about the porch. An instant of wild confusion ensued, then a frenzied mounting and riding. As thoroughly surprised as had been the first group were the raiders. Not waiting to learn the number of their attackers, they drove their spurs home and went away from there; but they took the burlapped bundles with them, all but one.

Rance hit the ranch-house door with a big shoulder and barged into the room. Grim tragedy was in the making there.

To one side, head up, fearless, stood Gypsy Carvel facing two flashily dressed Mexicans.

"You double-cross!" one was raging. "You betray! You sell us to Zorrilla! Die!"

A pearl-handled gun flashed down and roared!

But it was a dead hand that pulled the trigger. Even before Gypsy Carvel crumpled up in a pathetic little heap, the Mexican pitched forward, Rance Hatfield's bullet through his heart.

The other Mexican whirled, gun spouting flame. He knocked Rance's hat from his head, ripped the sleeve of his shirt, and died! Rance slammed his smoking guns into their holsters, leaped across the two bodies and gathered Gypsy in his arms.

Blood was streaming over the girl's face. Rance ripped the handkerchief from about his neck and mopped the worst of it away. He drew a deep and quivering breath of relief when he traced the flow to a jagged furrow amid the dark curls.

"Jest creased, or I don't know nothin' 'bout gun wounds!" he muttered. "Bleedin' like hell, though, and needs lookin' after."

Somewhere nearby a woman was screaming, or rather squawking like a chicken with its tail caught under a gate. Rance roared a stream of Spanish. The squawking ended in a cut-off screech as if said chicken had been grabbed by the neck. Something resembling a baby-elephant-stood-on-end came lurching from an inner room.

"*Madre de Dios*! *Maldito*! *Cien mil diablos*!" screeched the apparition, which Rance saw was the Mexican cook.

"Shut up!" he bawled at her. "Get hot water, and bandages! Move, *muy pronto*!"

The Mexican woman moved, still calling on all the saints and most of the devils. Rance picked

Gypsy up and laid her on a nearby couch. She was still unconscious, but color was coming back in her lips and cheeks. Her breathing was regular.

With slim, capable fingers he cleansed and bandaged the wound.

"That'll do till I can get a doctor," he told the cook. "I'm ridin' to town for one right now. You lock the door and get a shotgun. Don't let nobody in until I get back. Wheah's them two cowboys what ride for this spread?"

"They in town," mumbled the Mexican woman. "Yes'day payday. *La Senorita* tell 'em go!"

Rance gazed at the unconscious form of *La Senorita* and his black brows knit.

"Uh-huh," he mused. "Looks like she wanted to get 'em outa the way for t'night. Now if this ain't a mess!"

At the foot of the steps he stumbled over the burlapped bundle the raiders had missed. He knew what it contained before he unwrapped it.

"Good guns, too," he muttered, examining the long-barreled rifles by the light of a match. "Wonder how many more of these are holed up somewheah in Brazos? Plenty, I bet."

It was early afternoon when Rance got back to the Lazy-E with Doc McChesney. The cook let off one barrel of the shotgun at them as they dismounted.

"Damn lucky for us she didn't wait until we got to the steps," grunted the old doctor. "Chances are she woulda winged us anyhow if she'd had buckshot. Yell a little louder and mebbe she'll save the other ca'tridge."

Rance finally made the Mexican woman understand who it was; but she kept the shotgun aimed through the window until a weak but clear voice called peremptory orders from the inner room.

"Guess them punchers is still in town drunk," said Rance.

They found Gypsy in bed and pretty sick. Rance, worried and angry, spoke before she could:

"Gun runnin's a mighty pore bus'ness for any lady to mix inter, ma'am!"

There was a surprised, hurt look in the dark eyes that met his so steadily. Then they flashed scornfully.

"No worse than killing for pay," she replied, her voice little more than a whisper.

Rance glared at her, opened his mouth to speak, closed it again. For another moment green and brown eyes clashed, neither giving the breadth of a lash; then the brown faltered behind their silken curtain. The red lips that had set so stubbornly trembled. Rance drew a deep breath and fumbled with his hat. Shrewd old Doc McChesney glanced from one to the other and smiled a frosty smile under his moustache.

"Now that you two are finished tellin' each other what's what, mebbe I can give the patient a little lookin' over," he remarked dryly. "Rance, you git out till I send for you."

That night Doc McChesney sat thoughtfully in his little office. Finally he opened a small but strongly constructed safe and from one of the pigeonholes took a wooden box with a sliding lid. Printed on the lid were the words—

"The bullet that killed Jim Carvel."

Doc turned the battered leaden pellet over and over, his keen old eyes brooding. He had dug that bullet from Carvel's body when he performed the autopsy in his role of coroner.

He returned the slug to its place and carefully locked the safe, muttering disjointed sentences beneath his moustache—

"When the right time comes . . . lucky I saved that hunk o' lead . . . had a notion it might come in handy some time . . . make a fine pair . . . don't want nothin' standin' in the way. . . ."

24

Rance Hatfield was also doing some serious thinking. Not all of his thoughts were pleasant.

"What that gang had in mind ain't hard to figger," he reasoned. "They was gonna leave the rifles at the Lazy-E ranch-house—I got a hunch *she* didn't have no clear notion what was in them bundles—then somebody was gonna pick the bundles up and move 'em on somewheah. Them jiggers were Carvorca's men, all right. The other bunch somehow or other got wind of what was goin' on and aimed to wideloop the guns for themselves. Seems to me I've heard tell of a bandit below the Line named Zorrilla, come to think on it. Cavorca's men figgered Gypsy had doublecrossed them and went for her. What's puzzlin' me, though, is wheah they took them guns to. They didn't circle back nawth with 'em I know. Wheah in hell *did* they go? Guess I'd better ride down again and see if I can pick up a trail."

Then a little later, "Sho' is nice to heah Doc say she waren't hurt much!"

Rance rode south the next day. Before him, closer and closer, loomed the somber wall of the Black Hell hills. Close beneath the beetling cliffs he rode, searching with keen eyes for some cleft or canyon or gorge, and finding none. He picked up the trails of the scattered raiders, found where they converged and headed south. A mile from the cliff base the trail petered out, lost in a jumble of boulders and flinty soil. Rance was baffled.

Late in the afternoon he turned back and set out on a long slant that would eventually bring him to the Brazos trail not far from the Lazy-E ranchhouse. He was a thousand yards or so from the cliff base and passing a grove of cottonwoods.

Cr-r-rack!

Rance felt the wind of the bullet that split the air close to his head. Faint and thin, bedevilled by a myriad echoes, the report of the distant rifle reached him.

Crouching low, he spurred away from the ominous cliffs. The whining slug had come from there, or from the western tip of the grove. A puff of dust where it struck the ground farther on told him the direction.

"Next time I ride this way I'm bringin' a long gun along," he growled. "Sixes ain't no good when the other jigger is holed up in the rocks or behind a tree half-a-mile away."

Alert and watchful, he entered the grove, following a faint trail that wound among the trees. A thick carpet of leaves and mold muffled his horse's hoofs until they were almost soundless. It also muffled the tread of another horse that abruptly rounded a turn a scant dozen yards ahead.

Rance's right-hand gun came out of its sheath in a blue blur of movement; then, almost as swiftly, it dropped back into the holster. Rance pulled the black to a halt and lounged loosely in the saddle, eyes cold, lips set in a tight line.

Gypsy Carvel appeared as surprised as was the Ranger. Her horse faltered an instant under a checking rein, caught his stride and shuffled forward again. Gypsy pulled him up within arm's length of the black. She regarded the Ranger with cool hostility, pointedly appraising the quickly drawn and re-holstered Colt.

"What's the matter? Lose your nerve?" she asked.

Rance flushed under the implication, but his slow drawl was quietly undisturbed.

"See yore carryin' a rifle, ma'am. Looks like a powh'ful little gun with a mighty long range."

"It is," she replied evenly.

"Uh-huh, oughta carry plumb ac'rate from this end of the trees to down opposite that white-faced cliff back theah."

The girl regarded him wonderingly. "Just what are you driving at?" she asked.

Rance suddenly reached out a long arm and took the rifle from her. Before she had time to protest, he inserted the tip of his little finger into the muzzle and twisted it. The finger came out smudged. Rance handed the rifle back. Gypsy took it, her eyes big with astonishment.

"Ma'am," said the Ranger softly, "heah's a little tip that may come in handy some time—when you drygulch somebody, be sho' and clean yore gun right away; don't wait till you get home; it ain't safe. And another little thing—that rifle of yores shoots jest a mite high. Keep that in mind and pull her down a bit the next time."

He touched the stallion with a spur, rode around her and vanished amid the growth.

For long minutes Gypsy Carvel stared after him, her face slowly whitening. With trembling fingers she drew a freshly killed rabbit from her saddlebag and stared at where a high-power rifle bullet had ripped the back of its head away.

Rance rode to Brazos in a black mood. He glowered at the color-splashed sprawl of the mining town from a-top a rise. There was a queer tightening ache in his throat, a bitter taste in his mouth.

"Hell but she hates me!" he rasped aloud. "If I don't get drunk t'night and shoot somebody it'll be a wonder. Sho' wish Cavorca and his gang would come ridin' inter town t'night. I craves action!"

Before the night was over he got it, and Manuel Cavorca played his part in the near-riot.

"She's sho' boomin' t'night," Rance muttered as he shouldered his way along crowded Crippled

Cow street. "Why all the excitement, feller?" he asked a hilarious miner.

"New strike!" whooped the other. "Bunch o' the boys brought in pokes stuffed with red gold this aft'noon. Fust red gold ever turned up in this deestrict. It's the biggest thing since Forty-nine!"

Rance learned more about the new strike as the evening wore on. East of the old diggings, where nobody had even panned color before, the miners declared it was a virgin field. Men who had poured out of the town during the past few days to stake claims were now pouring back in to celebrate. Most of them were bringing sacks of dust with them. There were nuggets, too.

"It's the Mother Lode, that's what it is!" declared old-timers.

Rance ate a square meal, had several drinks and felt better. "I'm takin' a night off," he informed nobody in particular, unless it was himself. "I ain't gonna do no worryin' 'bout train robbers and war starters and gun slingin' females. I'm gonna enjoy myself for a while!"

There was diversion a-plenty in Brazos. Rance bucked the tiger for a while, lost quite a few dollars, and won them back with heavy interest at poker. He felt the need of another drink and took a couple more so the first one wouldn't feel lonesome. Several cowboys recognized in him a kindred spirit and they made it a party.

"Lesh all go over t' Cristobal's," said one of the punchers. "Mushic theah!"

"Thash a greaser hangout," objected another.

"Whacha differensh," defended the first speaker. "Some greasersh mighty fine fellers."

Cristobal's dance-hall-and-saloon was one of the biggest in town. There were many Mexicans there and a fair sprinkling of cowboys and miners. Cristobal, fat and oily, with a bland smile that never climbed up to his heavy-lidded eyes, presided back of the ornate bar. Unlike most of the Brazos saloons, Cristobal's was dimly lighted. The shadows thronging about the roof beams and in the corners lent an air of mystery and glamour. The music was the shivery wail of muted violins and softly thrummed guitars. A darkly handsome Mexican with a voice like rain-drops falling on silver bells sang the haunting, wistful ballads of the land of *manana*—

*"Oh, that I should have to leave you
 now!"*

And—

*"On the wings of the morning I come to
 you,
"My love!"*

Rance Hatfield glowered at the singer and called for whiskey.

One of the half-drunk punchers made a suggestion: "That Mex pizen, *tequila*, is a hell of a sight stronger, podner!"

"All right," growled Rance, "make her *tequila*! Drink up, you work dodgers, we're havin' another round!"

"Show me a grave where sleepeth my dearest love!"

"Damn!" rasped the Ranger, banging his empty glass on the bar. The crowd in Cristobal's grew thicker. The long bar was lined two deep. Perspiring bartenders knocked the necks off of bottles from which they had no time to draw the corks. They sloshed the raw liquor into glasses that impatient patrons pounded on the bar, or bawled for waiters to take them to the dancers and card players. The musicians opened their collars and fiddled madly. Dark-eyed *senoritas* with roses in their hair and swirling short skirts glided by, casting languorous glances at their partners or somebody else's partner. A softly seductive waltz dreamed to a close and the guitars began to lilt a fandango.

"Me, I'm gonna dance," one of the cowboys in Rance's party informed all and sundry.

A sinuous dark girl with great flashing eyes and a wealth of glossy black hair swirled up to Rance.

"Weeth me, tall *senor*?" she questioned.

"Why not," said the Ranger, sweeping her into his long arms.

Like a flower adrift in the wind, the girl floated across the crowded floor, her tiny slim feet seeming to glide on cushions of air. Rance

Hatfield, light-stepping with the poise of pliant long muscles and perfect condition, matched her grace. The other dancers began to draw away from the pair, pausing to watch, clipping out terse words of applause. Soon Rance and the girl had the center of the floor to themselves.

"*Senor*, you are most wonderful," she breathed.

"You ain't so bad yourself," drawled Rance.

And then there sounded a laugh, a silvery mocking laugh that spilled through the music and the murmurs like water through sand. Rance stiffened at the sound, faltered, lost a step and barely saved his partner from falling. His face flushed darkly red.

"*Caramba!*" hissed the Mexican girl, casting her glazing glare around the chuckling room.

Into the open space drifted another dancing couple. The man was tall and slim and amazingly graceful. He wore a beautifully embroidered velvet jacket with velvet pantaloons to match, a costume that served well to show off his supple, well-knit figure. His shirt front was a snowy foam of exquisite Mexican lace. His *sombrero*, pulled low over his eyes, was heavy with gold. A scarlet *serape* swept back over his shoulders with the gallant sway and stream of the tartans of a Scottish chief. Between *sombrero* and muffling *serape*, little could be seen of his face other than the gleam of startlingly white skin and the flash of eyes dark in the hat brim's shadow.

"All steel and hickory," muttered Rance Hatfield, his eyes narrowing as they shifted to the girl.

If Rance's panther-like little *senorita* was a flower drifting in the arms of the wind, the stranger's partner was the silver-shod wind itself stepping from rosebud to rosebud on fairy feet. She wore the plain, efficient costume of the western cowgirl, but she wore it as a queen wears the trappings of a throne. Her lips were scarlet as the roses the Mexican girls twined in their hair. Her tossing dark curls glowed with glints of sunlight. Back of the impish, mocking light in her great brown eyes were a sifting of dreams and the clean warmth of the wide, free rangelands.

"Damn! she sho' don't look like a girl what would drygulch a feller from behind a tree!" growled the Ranger, his face hardening at the thought.

So thoroughly had Gypsy Carvel filled his thoughts, he had given her handsome partner little more than a casual glance. Others, however, were paying much more attention to the stranger.

Cristobal, the fat, sinister proprietor of the *cantina*, summoned one of his lookouts with a barely perceptible motion of his head. He clipped a terse order, his cold eyes never leaving the dancing couple. The lookout sauntered unobtrusively to the back door and slipped out. As the door closed behind him, a pistol barrel crunched against his skull and he slumped to the ground, a senseless, bleeding heap. Cristobal, still intent on the tall stranger, did not know that.

Men were drifting casually into the saloon, dark-faced men with hats drawn low and guns swinging on their hips. They seemed to wander about aimlessly, but when they finally settled down to drinking or chatting or watching the games or the dancing, each man was in a strategic position that commanded a section of the big room.

Gypsy Carvel appeared to be thoroughly enjoying her dance and the sensation she and her partner had created. Rance Hatfield, glowering against the bar, a glass of *tequila* in his hand, failed to notice how often her glance strayed in his direction. As he tossed off the fiery liquor at a gulp and called for another one, the smile left the girl's lips and she frowned slightly; and when he drew the little Mexican *senorita*'s hand onto his arm, a look came into Gypsy Carvel's eyes that a woman would have had little trouble interpreting.

Abruptly her partner guided her to one side. He shoved her back against the railing of the little platform the musicians occupied.

"Stay there!" he commanded in a voice that sounded above the strum of the guitars. "Hold it!" he ordered the players.

The music stopped. The other dancers, who had been whirling about the cleared center space, paused uncertainly. The stranger strode to the middle of the room. His voice rang sharply.

"Cristobal!"

The cold-eyed proprietor went backward off his stool like an acrobat. He came to his feet, catlike, a sawed-off shotgun in his hands.

The stranger's white hand flashed to his belt. Across the room darted a lance of light to center on Cristobal's throat. He fell forward, dropping the shotgun, clawing at the bar over which blood spouted from the gaping knife wound in his throat. One of his bartenders grabbed the fallen shotgun and let go with both barrels.

The charge blew the stranger's *sombrero* from his head and tore out the upper sash of a window. The stranger, his golden hair gleaming in the lamp light, shot with his left hand and the bartender went down, screaming hoarsely. As if the shot had touched off hidden triggers, the walls of the room seemed to bulge outward with the roar of six-shooters.

"Carvorca! Cavorca!" bellowed the dark-faced men who had strolled so carelessly into the room. "*El Gran General* Manuel!"

Rance Hatfield swung the little *senorita* over the bar and dropped her behind the heavy oak, out of harm's way. Then he whirled to face Manuel Cavorca, who was shooting with both hands.

The bandit leader's men were hurling slugs

through the mirrors, smashing the tables and wrecking the place in general. Men and women spewed through the doors and windows like rabbits from a ferret-raided warren. Their howls and screams added to the bedlam of sound. Cristobal's *cantina* was being most thoroughly "taken apart!"

But Cristobal's retainers were more than mere waiters, bartenders, swampers and musicians. They had been hired for their efficiency with gun and knife. Recovered from their first paralysis of surprise, they were fighting it out with Cavorca's men. The crackle of six-shooters became a regular drumfire. Yells, curses, shrieks and groans soared up to the roof beams and bounced about like echoes of demons on a drunk. Outside sounded the deep roar of the crowd attracted by the battle.

Rance Hatfield fought his way through the riot toward Cavorca, striving at the same time to keep an eye on Gypsy Carvel. The girl crouched beside the musicians' stand, her eyes wide with horror, her face white.

"She never figgered on anythin' like this," panted the Ranger, smashing a man with his gun barrel and shooting another who was throwing down on him with a Colt.

Men were boiling through the front door. Cavorca gave them a glance and bellowed an order. He had recognized others of dead

Cristobal's followers. His own men began to sweep toward the back door.

Rance got through the battling crowd at last. Cavorca saw him coming, his pearl-handled guns came up, lined with the Ranger's breast.

Rance shot as swiftly as he could pull trigger. One of the silver-mounted sixes spun from Cavorca's hand as if it had grown wings. Bullets whipped through the gaudy *serape*. Cavorca slewed and weaved and ducked, his remaining Colt spouting flame. From the close-packed group by the back door went up a cry:

"Ze Ranger! It ees ze Ranger! Keel! Keel!"

A storm of lead blasted toward Rance. He saw blood suddenly spout from Cavorca's left arm, heard the bandit's scream of rage and pain. Then something struck him a sledge-hammer blow in the chest. Blood poured from his mouth and nose. He choked, gasped, strangled, the big Colts dropped from suddenly useless hands, his legs turned to water and he sank to the floor.

Manuel Cavorca, livid rage wiping all the unearthly beauty from his face and making it hideous, leaped forward, gun jutting.

Dimly through a bloody mist, Rance saw a little figure hurtle in front of the bandit, beating at his breast with tiny sun-goldened hands.

"No, Manuel, no I will hate you forever if you do! You lied to me, Manuel! You lied to me!"

Men surged across the room. Cavorca swept

the girl aside, turned and leaped through the back door. Rance Hatfield felt a soft arm pillowing his head, saw two great dark eyes in a white little face close to his, and was swallowed up in a blood-edged cloud of blackness.

25

Rance came back to his senses with a bandaged chest, an aching head and old Doc McChesney sitting beside his bed.

"Yore punctured," Doc told him, "but not so turr'ble serious. Bullet went through high and didn't do much damage 'sides from damn neah chokin' you to death with blood. If it hadn't been for that little Carvel girl, jedgin' from what I can gather of the ruckus, 'bout now you'd be listenin' to Saint Peter say, 'Jest step below, please'."

"Wheah'd she go, Doc?" Rance whispered.

"Home," said Doc, "after sittin' up the rest of the night and most of the day with you. Wouldn't leave till she was sho' I waren't lyin' when I told her theah waren't nothin' to worry 'bout."

Rance digested that for some time, and asked another question. "Doc, what was she doin' theah with Cavorca?"

Doc grunted and stuffed his pipe with tobacco before replying.

"Well," he said when the pipe was going good, "from what I can jedge, Cavorca fooled her proper. He told her he jest wanted her to go to Cristobal's and dance with him. Said that he would be safe theah, and anyway he would keep his face covered. Of co'hse his idea was to hold ev'body's attention to the dancin' till his men could sift in and get placed. When Gypsy saw you in theah she jest 'bout passed out, but by then theah waren't nothin' for her to do but go through with it. You and the little Mex gal puttin' on a show right at that time played inter Cavorca's hand. The Carvel gal, incident'ly, seems to have sorta took a dislike to that little Mex. I sho' b'lieve she's offa Cavorca for good this time, though."

"But why did Cavorca wanta wipe out Cristobal?" asked Rance.

" 'Cause it was Cristobal's men what raided that gun runnin' party of Cavorca's. Cristobal was workin' for Zorrilla, who's stagin' the rev'lution over in Chihuahua."

"All clear as a waterhole with a hawg wallerin' in it," admitted Rance. "Exceptin' one thing," he added. "Doc, how in hell do them jiggers get acrost the Line and back like they do? They sho' don't use the Canyon Trail, and theah ain't no other that I know of."

"Past me," grunted Doc. "Mebbe they're so clost to bein' angels they're sproutin' wings and flyin' over the cliffs. Now you shet up and go to sleep soon as I've fed you some soup. Yore tough as a steer's hide and if you do what I tell you to, you'll be ridin' again in six weeks."

Rance fooled him. He was riding in half that time, although Doc did not approve of it.

"You bust that hole loose 'fore she's healed proper and you'll have trouble," the old physician cautioned him. "And inc'dentally, I heard that you laid Cavorca up for a spell with a busted shoulder, so what's yore hurry?"

"A little thing like a busted shoulder ain't gonna stop Cavorca," Rance assured him gloomily. "I betcha he's twirlin' his loop right now and when it settles, somebody's gonna get yanked clean outa the hull."

Rance was right. Like a thunderbolt Cavorca struck. Silver City felt the weight of his hand first. The stage bearing the Alhambra mines payroll and guarded by two special deputies and a Ranger was raided. The Ranger and one of the deputies died. The Alhambra payroll went to Mexico. Cavorca, his left arm strapped to his breast, his bridle between his teeth and a silver-mounted Colt in his right hand, led his men.

Soon after came disquieting news from below the Line. "The revolutionary, Cavorca, attacked a detachment of *El Presidente*'s soldiers and annihilated it," said the dispatch. Adding with Mexican laconism, "No prisoners were taken!"

Rance Hatfield's lean jaw tightened even more. "This side the border'll catch it next," he predicted.

Wails and protests began to drift in from outlying ranches and settlements. Cavorca had run cattle off here. He had burned and murdered there. He was expected daily at another place. Captain Morton sent Rance an urgent message.

"For the love of Pete, try and do something," wrote the captain. "People all over the state are pannin' the Rangers 'cause they can't be in a dozen places at once. The governor is thinking seriously of asking Washington for troops. If he gets them it will make things all the worse, and it'll end the Rangers. If you can only grab off Cavorca! Without his brains at the head of it, the whole business'll bust up like a puff of smoke outside a gun barrel."

Rance watched the Canyon Trail day and night, and while he was watching it, a band of Cavorca's men rode into Brazos, wrecked a saloon owned by the brother of the dead Cristobal, cut the brother's throat and vanished in the night.

"They headed straight south, acrost the Lazy-E cattle ranch," a cowboy declared to Rance. "I follered them a ways, and hightailed back to town when one of 'em creased my cayuse with a slug."

Grim of mouth and eye, the Ranger rode to the Lazy-E ranch-house. The Mexican cook admitted him. Gypsy Carvel received him coldly.

"I have not seen Manuel since that night in Brazos," she said. "I never want to see him again. He used me as a dupe and double-crossed me. No, I have no idea how he crossed the Line so quickly. I wouldn't tell you if I did know."

"I heahd tell Cavorca's Yaquis and half-breeds

shot a woman and stole a girl baby in that raid on the Bowtie spread over east of heah," Rance said softly.

The girl's face whitened. Her voice trembled.

"I—I heard that, too." She leaned forward earnestly and looked the Ranger in the eye: "Believe me, please, I really do not know the way through the hills. Manuel never told me, and he never used it in the daytime. It is a secret known only to him and his men and their like."

Rance rode away from the Lazy-E ranch-house in a decidedly mixed frame of mind. Gypsy Carvel had followed him onto the porch and hesitated a question:

"You—you intend to keep on looking for the secret trail?"

"I sho' do," Rance assured her as he swung into the saddle.

"I fear you are exposing yourself to terrible danger," she warned him earnestly. "I'm sure they guard that trail, day and night, and they are men who will stop at nothing."

Her round white little chin jutted forward defiantly. "And I want to tell you," she added, "although I don't suppose you'll believe me, I *did not* shoot at you that day you met me in the grove!"

A pleased grin twitched at the corners of Rance's mouth as he recalled that outburst.

"Darned if I don't b'lieve she was tellin' the

truth," he declared. "If she'd shot at me she wouldn't deny it, and the chances are plumb good she wouldn'ta missed, either. 'Sides, she jest nacherly ain't the kinda girl what would sneak up behind a feller and kick him in the belly when his back was turned. If she took a notion to do some shootin', she'd walk right straight up to yore face and plug you 'tween the eyes."

The grin left his face and his eyes became calculating. "And that means some horned toad was holed 'mong the rocks somewheah. I musta been gettin' sorta clost to their blasted trail if they felt they'd better start throwin' lead at me. Feller, we'll jest give them another chance to do some gun slingin'."

Slowly, keen eyes searching the rocks, he rode along the frowning wall.

"Theah's that big white-lookin' cliff I noticed that day," he mused. "Funny sorta outcroppin', ain't it? Kinda shines now it's gettin' dark. Yeah, it was jes 'bout heah I purty neah stopped that slug."

Once again the Ranger rode along close to the cliffs, scanning every inch of them and finding nothing. Abruptly he turned the black horse and rode across the prairie until he was a mile or more from the hills.

For a long time he sat studying the cliffs, plotting their position in relation to the higher mountains to the north.

"That old bald-headed feller t'other side of Brazos is right in line with that big white cliff," he decided. "Now if I was on t'other side the cliffs and could keep a eye on his top, I got a hunch I'd hit the back-door end of that darned trail. It's wuth tryin', anyhow."

Near Brazos, Rance met Doc McChesney ambling along on his easy-going horse.

"Jest 'tendin' to a little chore," said Doc. "You look tuckered. Didn't I tell you to take it easy with that half-healed hole through you? Some jigger's gonna be pattin' you in the face with a spade if you don't slow up a bit."

Rance rode on to bed. Doc rode to the Lazy-E ranch-house. He found Gypsy at home.

"Met that long-legged galoot of a Ranger ridin' from this direction," he observed, accepting a cup of coffee, "did he stop heah?"

"He did not," Gypsy replied coldly.

"Any notion wheah he'd been?" asked Doc.

"I'm not in the least interested in his comings or goings," said Gypsy.

"Didn't look so well," remarked Doc casually. "Got a notion that bullet hole ain't healin' jest as it ought to. He'd oughta not be ridin' 'round so much."

"Is—isn't there some way to make him stop?" faltered the girl,

"Got a notion he might if you'd ask him to," countered Doc, giving her a shrewd glance.

"I—I couldn't do that," she breathed.

"Might save his life," remarked Doc.

There was a soft little gasp. Doc looked up quickly and saw tears on her dark lashes. His old face suddenly became all kindness.

Gypsy was crying openly now. "He—he killed my father! I—I hate him! At least I—I ought to hate him!"

"Jest s'posin' he *didn't* kill yore father?"

"Oh!" exclaimed the girl breathlessly. "Oh, what do you mean?"

Old Doc McChesney fumbled a little wooden box from his pocket and shook a battered lead pellet onto the table.

"That's yore dad's gun you carry, ain't it?" he asked. "Uh-huh, I thought so. What calibre is it?"

"Why it's a .32-20," replied the mystified girl.

"Uh-huh, a calibre that's darn scarce in this section o' country. You hardly ever run acrost one. Guess you know the Rangers don't carry nothin' but .45's. That's sho' what Rance Hatfield allus carries, ain't it?"

"I've never seen him with anything else," admitted Gypsy.

"No, nor nobody else," stated Doc emphatically. He handed her the battered bit of lead.

"Gypsy, that's the slug that killed yore dad," he told her.

"Oh!" exclaimed the girl, shuddering away

from it. "Why—why do you bring me the awful thing?"

Doc seemed to hesitate for words. "I ain't never been able to piece the whole story t'gether," he admitted, "but one thing I do know—*Rance Hatfield never shot yore dad.*"

"But—but his own report said he did!" gasped Gypsy.

"Uh-huh, but he didn't. The bullet what killed yore dad was shot from a .32-20 hawgleg, and Rance Hatfield carried .45's! I hate to tell you, Gypsy, but theah ain't no doubt 'bout it—yore Dad shot hisself. Mebbe he got sorry afterward and told Rance so 'fore he cashed in. Anyhow. Rance shouldered the blame and kept yore dad from goin' to a suicide's grave. If things had worked out different, I'd never said anythin' 'bout it to nobody, but the way things is, I figgered you oughta know."

For a long moment Gypsy Carvel sat staring at the battered bullet. "Poor old Daddy," she said at last. "He wanted to spare me—I know that was the way of it; and Rance helped him! Oh, Doc, think of the things I've said to him and how I've treated him! Will he—will he *ever* forgive me?"

26

Rance Hatfield rode northwest out of Brazos. Blanket and poncho were strapped behind his saddle. In the saddlebags was food. Rance was prepared for several days in the hills.

He reached the Canyon Trail and turned south. Then east into the gloomy fastness of the Black Hell hills. For two days he threaded his way among canyons and gorges, checking his position with the plainsman's uncanny sense of distances and directions. Late afternoon of the second day found him guiding his horse along a scrambling ridge, his eyes glancing frequently toward where, misty with distance, a huge rock-crested mountain loomed in the northern sky. That mountain was the "bald-headed old feller" Rance had lined with the white cliff the morning the two Mexicans had attempted to drygulch him.

"Onless we done played a bum hunch, it oughta be somewheah clost 'round heah," he told the horse. "Let's do some lookin', feller, and see if we can't find it."

Before the last light faded he did find it. "It" was a plainly marked trail winding away southward. Eyes vigilant, guns loose in their sheaths, Rance headed north along the trail.

Through canyons and gorges it wound, over steep ridges and along dizzy hogbacks. Soon after the sun vanished in a riot of scarlet and gold and burnished copper, a great white moon soared up over the hills to make the going possible.

Nearer and nearer loomed the giant buttresses of the cliff wall that battlemented the north extent of the Black Hell hills.

"Hoss, it sho' looks like yore gonna need wings to get over that," Rance declared. "I can't see a split in them cliffs nowheah."

With startling abruptness and a simplicity that disgusted the Ranger with himself, the mystery was solved. Right up to the base of a steeply sloping rocky hill ran the trail, and lost itself in the jagged face of a blacker shadow. Rance rode into the shadow and found himself in a fairly narrow passage, walled and roofed.

"A cave!" he grunted. "Jest a darned nacherel tunnel through the cliffs! But how in the blankety-blank bloomin' blue blazes does it open out on the nawth side of these rocks so that nobody can see it?"

Suddenly he pulled the black horse up. In his ears sounded Gypsy Carvel's warning—". . . guarded day and night!"

He had seen nothing of guards so far, but then they would have little reason to fear attack or discovery from the south. Where the cave opened through the cliff wall, if it really did open, would be the logical point for a guard to be stationed.

"We jest won't take no chances," decided Rance, heading the black horse toward a manzanita thicket a little distance from the trail.

He hobbled the bronk loosely and re-entered the cave on foot. The floor was soft with slippery mud and his passing created little or no sound.

Yard after yard he groped along through the black dark, testing each step before he trusted his weight upon it. Caves were tricky things and there might be pitfalls in this one, awaiting the unwary.

"Wonder how long this darn ditch-with-a-roof over it is, anyhow," he growled. "She's twistin' and squirmin' like a snake with the itch, too. I'm liable to meet myself comin' back most any minute now."

Water dripped continually from the roof and trickled down the rock walls. Rance shivered under the icy drops and quickened his pace a little. A dozen steps more and he slowed to a crawl.

There was a faint glow sifting through the dark ahead. Rance crept on, rounded a turn and blinked at a fire a scant dozen yards from where he stood.

The air felt different and the water had ceased dripping. Rance glanced up and saw a narrow strip of stars twinkling in a blue-black sky.

"Looks like I'm darn neah through," he

muttered, "and theah's the watchman, sho' as yore a foot high!"

Perched on a narrow shelf that commanded the narrow gorge into which the tunnel opened was a motionless figure. The man was facing north and apparently drowsing.

"Anybody headin' this way has to pass the fire," Rance deduced. "Then they're in plain sight 'fore they can see the guard. One man with a long gun can hold off a army."

Just as impossible would it be to slip past the fire going north. Rance crouched against the rock wall and thought furiously. He could see where a narrow track sloped upward to the guard's perch. It was steep and apparently strewn with loose stones. Rance shock his head gloomily as he measured the distance with his eye. Then he glided forward and went up the track with lithe, sure steps.

He covered half the distance. The guard had not moved. Two-thirds—and still he was undiscovered. Then his foot struck a loose stone and sent it crashing over the edge.

The guard leaped to his feet, whirled about. Rance could easily have shot him, but he feared the possible consequences of the report. For all he knew, there were other guards farther along the cleft. He covered the remaining distance in a panther-like rush and his hand closed on the Mexican's throat as his mouth opened to yell.

Down went the struggling pair. The guard's rifle was knocked from his hand to clatter on the rock floor a dozen feet below. Rance clamped a sinewy wrist just in time to stop the flickering thrust of a knife. He ground the man's knuckles against a jagged stone, the fingers writhed convulsively and the knife tinkled away. Rance let go his hold and whizzed a blow at the other's jaw.

The guard ducked his head aside and countered with a clawing slap. Rance lunged sideways to avoid it and over the edge went the battling pair.

The fall seemed a long one to Rance. Stars and jagged flames and writhing spears of light blazed before his eyes as he struck the rock. He felt his senses slipping. Black waves of darkness hovered over him. With a tremendous effort of the will he thrust them back and staggered to his feet.

The guard lay motionless where he had fallen, his head lolling grotesquely to one side.

"Busted his neck, sho' as hell," muttered the Ranger, rubbing a bleeding lump on the side of his own head. "Now what?"

From the blackness of the cave mouth sounded a faint clicking. Rance instantly recognized it for what it was—horses' striking the muddy floor. He went into whirlwind action.

Seizing the guard's body he stuffed it behind a convenient boulder, first stripping off the dirty *serape*. He retrieved the fellow's rifle and his wide *sombrero*. Draping the blanket around his shoulders and clapping the *sombrero* on his head, he raced up the stony track to the lookout's perch.

Nearer and nearer came the sound of horses. Rance could hear the jingle of bridles and the creak and pop of saddle leather. Low voices speaking. Spanish drifted to him.

"One slip, feller, and yore gonna grow yoreself wings in a hurry," he murmured. "Heah's sho' hopin' you figger the right thing!"

From the cave mouth rode horsemen. Rance took a chance and challenged them in Spanish: "*Alto ahi*. Halt where you are!"

The horses did not pause.

"It is we, thou stupid fool!" called an impatient voice. "Rub the sleep from your eyes and see that *El Gran General* rides in our midst. Remain you at your post until we return. Let no one pass."

Rance muttered unintelligible Spanish and grounded his rifle. He hunched back against the wall, fearful that the riders would note his greater height, but they paid him scant attention. He counted nine men besides Manuel Cavorca, who was talking earnestly with a man beside him.

The Ranger drew a deep breath of relief as the clicking hoofs died away in the gloom of the gorge. He waited a few minutes and hurried down from his perch.

Alert against the possibility of other guards, he eased along in the wake of the horsemen, but found none. The cleft turned sharply to the right and ran between walls that drew closer and closer together. Finally there was barely room for a single horseman to pass.

Abruptly the left-hand wall fell away and Rance found himself standing at the foot of a tall white cliff with the open prairie rolling northward before his eyes. Due north, hanging dimly in the sky, was the rocky crest of a huge mountain.

"Well, I'll be damfinoed!" grunted the Ranger. "No wonder nobody could see this hole by ridin' along the cliff. The rock sorta folds back on itself like a sheet of paper and looks like a bulge. 'Less a feller would walk right up to the cliff, he'd never 'spect theah was a hole heah. And theah goes Cavorca and his sidewinders!"

The horsemen were mere shadowy blotches on the prairie, heading north. As Rance gazed the grove swallowed them up.

Back through the gorge and the cave went the Ranger, as fast as his high-heeled boots would permit. He found his horse, mounted and rode swiftly northward.

"They're gonna run more guns t'night or I miss my guess a long ways," he told the cayuse. "Feller, this is our big chance to grab off Cavorca. All we got to do is locate him in Brazos."

Rance found Brazos booming as never before. The streets were crowded. Men lined the bars three deep. So many couples were on the dance floors that they could barely shuffle along. The gamblers were reaping a golden harvest. There were so many fights in progress the watchers got cross-eyed trying to see them all at once.

"What in blazes has come over this town, anyhow?" Rance asked a cowboy with a black eye, and a quart bottle in his hip pocket.

"Wheah you been all year, feller?" demanded the puncher. "Dontcha know it's Fourth of July—the day Columbus discovered Ameriky? We jest found it out and we're celebratin' bein' discovered. Have a drink?"

Rance had hoped to enlist the aid of the town marshal and possibly swear in a few special deputies; but the marshal was drunk and material for deputies was scarce as cowpokes in church. Rance gave up in disgust and devoted his entire attention to getting a line on Manuel Cavorca.

From saloon to saloon he went, drinking little and seeing much. He prowled the Mexican quarter from end to end, and found nothing. The night was growing steadily wilder and his chances of corralling Cavorca correspondingly less.

"Hell, I'll go see Doc McChesney," he finally decided. "Mebbe he can suggest somethin'."

Doc listened to Rance's story of the hidden trail without comment. The Ranger asked his advice and Doc gave it without hesitation.

"Looks like Cavorca smelled a rat, or

somethin'," he said. "He ev'dently figgered you might be on the lookout for him heah. If he really is figgerin' on runnin' guns t'night, I callate he's got 'em holed up somewheah outside the town. Don't fergit, too, he got raided by Zorrilla that fust time. Zorrilla is a tough *hombre* with brains and like as not he's got more friends heah 'sides Cristobal. Cavorca'll keep that in mind, too."

"Then you don't figger I got much chance of locatin' him heah in Brazos?"

"Nope," said Doc decidedly. "If you jest had a few men you could depend on, the proper idea would be to head him off 'tween heah and the border, now that you know which way he goes."

Rance started to his feet, his eyes brightening. "Doc, when it comes to brains yore the big lead bull of the herd. That notion of yores is plumb salty. I'll jest nacherly drop my loop on *Senor* Cavorca down to that hole through the hills. Doc, it'll be a pipe!"

"Who all you gonna take with you?" asked Doc.

Rance grinned. "Jest a coupla little fellers what can sho' talk loud," he replied, tapping his holsters. "I'd be plumb obliged for a rifle, though, if you got one to spare."

Doc bellowed protest and tried to talk Rance out of the venture.

"It's plumb suicide yore committin'," he declared. "How you gonna handle ten of them killers? They'll be loaded for bear and won't leave even a grease spot of you. Don't try it, Rance."

Finally, however, with much grumbling, he got the rifle and handed it to the Ranger.

"I'll amble out and look for flowers," he grunted. "Got any last words you wanta speak?"

27

Less than an hour after Rance had left, Doc had another visitor. Gypsy Carvel, white-faced, breathing hard, pounded on his door.

"Have you seen Rance Hatfield?" she demanded almost before Doc could get the door open.

"Sho', jest left heah," Doc told her.

"Where did he go? I must see him at once! Manuel Cavorca is in Brazos, looking for him."

"Sho' now, that makes it practic'ly unanimous," said Doc. "Rance is lookin' for Manuel."

"But Manuel intends to kill him!" wailed the girl.

"I don't callate Rance is plannin' on 'zactly kissin' Manuel," observed Doc.

"You don't understand," despaired Gypsy. "Manuel has his men with him, nine or ten of the worst. They are taking rifles across the Line tonight and they also intend to get rid of Rance for good.

"And that isn't all," she added. "Rosa, my cook, has friends in the Mexican quarter here in Brazos. She visited them today and they told her that the bandit Zorrilla is going to ambush Manuel somewhere and kill him and take the guns away from him."

"Well, now, that's plumb fine!" exclaimed Doc.

"If they'll jest manage it right and kill each other. I wonder wheah—"

His voice suddenly trailed away. "Oh, good gosh!" he muttered.

"What's the matter?" asked Gypsy, her eyes big with apprehension.

"It's Rance!" yammered Doc. "He'll be right in the middle of it. Hell, yes, that's the place Zorrilla'll drygulch Cavorca. He knows about that hole-in-the-wall too."

"What in the world are you talking about?" wailed Gypsy.

Doc told her, as Rance had told him. The girl's breath caught as she listened.

"Yes," she gasped, "they'll be waiting for Manuel in the cave. Rance will ride right into their midst and they will kill him. He won't have a chance!"

"Looks that way," agreed Doc dully.

Gypsy dashed for the door.

"Hey, wheah you goin'?" yelled Doc.

"I'm going to warn Rance," she called back as the door slammed.

Old Doc McChesney got creakily to his feet. "Damn this rheumatism, anyway!" he gritted. "I'll never be able to ride that far, but I'm gonna do it anyhow. Wheah in hell is my hawgleg?"

Rance wasted no time getting to the cave. "I gotta make it 'fore daylight," he repeated over and over, anxiously scanning the eastern sky for the first streaks of dawn. "If they see me 'fore I get holed up, they'll cut and run for it and if Cavorca has his reg'law they'll make a clean getaway."

He sighed with relief as the shimmering white cliff hove into view. It still lacked nearly an hour until dawn. After debating the matter for a moment, he tethered the black horse in a convenient thicket and entered the cleft on foot.

"I'll jest hang 'round the front door heah till they show up this side the grove," he decided. "That'll give me plenty time to ease back into the cave and line on them as they start comin' in. 'Spect I better slip back and build up that fire a bit, too. They might get suspicious if it's out. 'Sides, it'll give me more light to shoot by if shootin' gets nec'sary."

The fire had burned down to a few almost cold embers. Rance got it going again with wood he found stacked nearby. Then he returned to the cleft mouth. He jerked his rifle up and lined the sights with a rider tearing across the stony belt that bordered the cliff wall.

"Who the—" he muttered. "Hell's fire and damnation!

"Gypsy, what you doin' heah!" he shouted, leaping into view.

The girl pulled her horse to a floundered halt. Her story came out in gasping words. Rance instantly grasped its significance.

"They'll have us comin' and goin'," he agreed. "We'd better get through to the other side this darned hole 'fore one or the other of them shows up."

"I'm afraid my horse is done for," said Gypsy.

"Looks it," nodded Rance. "Turn him into that thicket and we'll take a chance on them not seein' him when they pass."

His keen eyes searched the prairie to the north, shimmering ghostly gray in the strengthening dawn.

"Heah comes Cavorca and his outfit," he said. "See them little black dots jumpin' up and down jest east of the grove? Let's get goin'."

Walking swiftly but carefully they made their way into the cleft. They entered the cave, passed the now brightly burning fire and crept along through the black darkness. Suddenly he gripped the girl's arm; his keen ears had caught a small stealth sound somewhere in front.

"They're heah already!" he breathed.

Gypsy's whisper came back to him. "Yes, and I can hear horses behind us."

For an instant Rance felt the promptings of panic. Their situation was truly desperate. Hemmed between the rival bandit gangs, they had an excellent chance of being blasted out of existence by the first volley fired by either side. Frantically Rance groped along the dripping wall, seeking some source of concealment.

He found it, such as it was, a shallow, narrow crevice down which water trickled in a steady stream. Cautiously he guided the girl into it and squeezed his own broad shoulders in after her. They were completely hidden, with a foot or two to spare.

"These darn walls are all cracked and seamed," he explained. "Water in back of 'em, the chances are. Hill caves in this section is gen'rally that way. We stand a purty good chance of them passin' us up."

Tensely they waited. From the darkness ahead sounded stealthy shufflings. Then silence, broken only by the steadily loudening click of hoofs from the north.

Cavorca and his men were proceeding cautiously. The missing watchman evidently worried them. Rance felt sure from their steady though slow progress, however, that they did not yet suspect what was in store for them.

Without warning the darkness ahead belched fire and smoke. Yells and shrieks followed the withering blast of lead. The screams of stricken horses added to the hideous turmoil. Manuel Cavorca's clear voice rang above the tumult:

"Dismount! Take cover. Pedro, Guillermo, the flares!"

Bullets continued to storm out of the darkness. Now they were answered by flashes from where Cavorca's men hurled themselves to the cave floor. Rance heard the terrified horses thunder away toward the gorge.

A light flashed up, soared through the blackness in a flaming arc and dropped to the floor. It blazed high, a ball of oil soaked rags, making the scene as bright as day.

Crouched behind a rude barricade of stones were a half score of *sombreroed* Mexicans. The light glinted on their rifle barrels. They blazed away at the remainder of Cavorca's bandits, who had taken to what scanty cover they could find—small boulders, jutting bulges of rock, shallow holes scooped in the mud. Several quiet forms lay in the space between.

"The Cavorca gang caught hell the first crack," breathed Rance, peeping cautiously around the edge of his slanting crevice.

The rifles were rolling a regular drumfire. Bullets plunked into the mud, smashed against the walls and caromed from the roof. Yells and curses went up as a hit scored. Cavorca's voice sounded, encouraging his men.

"Don't look like the bullet's run what can do for that hellion," muttered Rance. "Well, we'll see. Wonder what he's got up his sleeve? He keeps tellin' his men to hold on a minute longer."

The flare was burning low. Something trailing a stream of sparks went hurtling through the smoke.

"That one ain't gonna light," muttered Rance. "It—"

Cr-r-rash!

A terrific explosion rocked the cave. In the instant of blinding glare, Rance saw the bodies of Zorrilla's drygulchers fly in every direction.

"Dynamite!" gasped the Ranger. "Cavorca threw a stick of dynamite among 'em! If he ain't—"

The words were wiped from his lips by a second terrific growling crash. The very cliffs seemed to rock and reel as great masses of stone came thundering down upon the cave floor. There sounded a horrified shriek that was chopped off as if cut with a knife. For another moment the terrific crashes continued as more and more rocks broke loose. Silence followed, then low mutterings.

28

Rance could hear men creeping about in the darkness. A light flared and another. A voice rose in terror.

"The cave it is blocked, at both ends! We are dead men!"

Manuel Cavorca's voice sounded, clear, fearless: "Steady, you fool. This is no time to let yourself go. We'll dig out some way."

Rance nodded to himself in the dark. "Ev'body's gotta work t'gether this time," he grunted. His voice rose:

"Cavorca!"

"Yes?" replied the bandit leader. "Who's calling?"

A fresh flare blazed up, disclosing Cavorca and three of his men still on their feet. The Zorrilla drygulchers were crushed under tons of rock. Rance stepped out of the crevice, rifle at the ready.

"Well I'll be damned!" exploded Cavorca. "The Ranger! What the hell you doing here?"

"Oh, I come along without a invite," Rance told him. "Question is, how we gonna get out?"

Cavorca shrugged. "Looks like we are not," he admitted. "Looks like you and I have run a dead heat. We—good God! Gypsy!"

Rance slipped a long arm about the girl's slim waist. "Looks like we jest gotta get out some way," he said.

One of Cavorca's men spoke up: "*Capitan*, I am sure the rock fall at this end is of no great thickness. Over there where you hurled the dynamite is where most of it came down."

Rance laid the rifle aside and strode to where the jumble of splintered stone extended from floor to roof.

"We ain't got anythin' much to work with," he said, "but we might as well make a try at it."

"Must hurry, too," added Cavorca. "Water is seeping in here fast, and there isn't any too much air to breathe, either."

They went to work, levering masses of stone loose with rifle barrels. Clawing away the muck and the smaller fragments, Rance felt confident they had not far to go.

It was the water that worried them most. It rose steadily, seeping through the crumbly wall in a dozen places. Part of the wall was little more than loosely packed shale and earth. Here a stream poured steadily, growing in size as the minutes passed and more and more of the spongy mass sluffed off. Rance gave it many anxious glances.

"Theah's a whole darn river back o' that mud," he told Cavorca. "If she busts loose we won't have no more chance than a rat in a rain barrel."

As they progressed the fallen rock became

packed tighter. Soon they were loosening the fragments with great difficulty. The water kept coming faster.

Gypsy suddenly screamed. A whole section of the rubbly wall had sluffed away. A torrent of water gushed through the crevice. More and more of the wall dissolved under the pressure.

Rance hurled fragments of rock into the opening. They were swept away almost as fast as he threw them.

"They ain't big enough!" he panted. "We need somethin' long and heavy to hold the water back till we can build the wall up again."

He was shoved aside. Manuel Cavorca wedged his tall, broad-shouldered body into the crevice.

"Here is something long and heavy," he gasped, his face whitening with the strain. "Quick, build up around me with rocks and mud!"

"Feller, you can't do that!" protested Rance. "Yore liable to be crushed to death any minute!"

Cavorca's unbelievably handsome face contorted.

He lapsed into his accustomed tongue, Spanish.

"Do as I say! It is not our worthless life of which I think! It is for my cousin, my only friend, I do this. Hurry!"

"Right!" the Ranger barked. "Feller if you go out, you'll go out like a man!"

With rocks and muck they walled him in, up to his laboring chest, almost to his shoulders. The water still gushed through, but the wall ceased to sluff off. Rance and two of the Mexicans went back to the barrier, leaving one man to fight the water flow. They found the fallen rocks almost immovable.

"We gotta blast a hole through," said Rance. "Is theah any more dynamite?"

"No," replied one of the Mexicans, "there was but one steeck!"

"Hafta use powder then," decided the Ranger. "Pull the bullets outa ca'tridges and make a pile. Keep it dry."

While the Mexicans jerked the bullets loose with their teeth, Rance made a hole for the charge, carefully lining it with bits of dry rock. He formed it deep in a crack between two huge fragments, where the powder would exert its full force. From time to time he glanced to where Manuel Cavorca stood crucified in the crevice. Blood was trickling down the bandit's mouth. His face was gray with suffering; but he stood like a figure of stone.

"Bad—bad all the way through," muttered the Ranger, "but he's got the guts of a man, I'm tellin' the world!"

"The powder she is ready," called one of the Mexicans. "You will need a fuse."

"Wet a strip of cloth, rub powder on it and twist it," Rance ordered. "Let's have that powder."

With the greatest care he placed the charge,

tamping it down, wedging the makeshift fuse in place with bits of rock.

"All right," he told the Mexicans, "take the *senorita* back with you as far as you can go. I'm gonna touch her off."

The girl protested tearfully. "Rance, if that fuse doesn't burn right you'll be blown to pieces."

"Manuel's takin' his chance," replied the Ranger. "I gotta take mine."

"Let me light it, Rance!"

Rance gestured to the Mexicans. "Get goin' *hombres*, take her back."

Still protesting, Gypsy was hurried as far from the charge as possible. Rance set his jaw grimly and struck a match. If the fuse burned too fast—!

He touched the match to the twisted strip. It smoldered, sputtered. The fire raced along it.

Rance hurled himself away, striving madly to get at least some distance from the explosion. The powder let go before he was a dozen feet from the fallen roof.

He was swept from his feet and smashed against the muddy floor. His ears rang to the roar, his senses reeled. He was showered with fragments of rock that cut and bruised him.

Almost beside him sounded a groaning sigh. Manuel Cavorca pitched headlong from the crevice, blood pouring from his mouth. Over him rushed a torrent of water.

"Outside, quick! The way's clear!" yelled

Rance, snatching Cavorca from the water. "You all right, Gypsy?"

Through a ragged opening they scrambled, coughing in the powder fumes, fighting the rising water. Rance held Cavorca with one arm and helped Gypsy with the other. Water was swirling through the cleft knee deep by the time they reached the outer air and sank panting and exhausted at the foot of the white cliff. Old Doc McChesney was just riding up.

Doc examined Cavorca briefly. "Done for," he stated. "Artery busted. Back too, I got a notion. Guess yore job is finished, Rance."

"Uh-huh," Rance nodded, "that ends the rev'lution and saves a border war."

He gazed down at the dead bandit still startlingly handsome despite the blood that streaked his face.

"Doc," he said softly, "somehow I got a notion the Big Boss of the Big Spread acrost the River ain't gonna be so turrible hard on a feller what cashed in his final chips savin' other folks's lives."

He turned to the three Mexicans, who stood staring sadly at their dead leader.

"You boys did yoreselves proud," he told them. "Hope you have good luck down in *manana* land."

"Thank you, *senor*," they replied simply. "We wish you and your lovely *senorita* all happiness."

"Ain't so sho' she's mine," muttered Rance, "but I'm sho' hopin'."

"I see you still got yore arm 'round her, and she sho' ain't makin' no fight to bust loose!" grunted old Doc.

Gypsy blushed, and snuggled a little closer.

Books are produced in the United States using U.S.-based materials

Books are printed using a revolutionary new process called THINKtech™ that lowers energy usage by 70% and increases overall quality

Books are durable and flexible because of Smyth-sewing

Paper is sourced using environmentally responsible foresting methods and the paper is acid-free

Center Point Large Print
600 Brooks Road / PO Box 1
Thorndike, ME 04986-0001 USA

(207) 568-3717

US & Canada:
1 800 929-9108
www.centerpointlargeprint.com